The Last Laugh

The Last Laugh

A MYSTERY BY

John R. Riggs

DEMBNER BOOKS · NEW YORK

Dembner Books
Published by Red Dembner Enterprises Corp.,
1841 Broadway, New York, N.Y. 10023
Distributed by W. W. Norton & Company, Inc.,
500 Fifth Avenue, New York, N.Y. 10110

Library of Congress Cataloging in Publication Data
Riggs, John R., 1945–
    The last laugh.

    I. Title.
PS3568.I372L3   1984   813'.54   83-20921
ISBN 0-934878-37-4

To Pat Gammon and Mom and Pop.
Thanks for all your help.

THE LAST LAUGH

C H A P T E R 1

Si Buckles was dead. No question about it. Si Buckles was dead. He was my age, forty, and with his ruddy skin and boyish smile that made him look like a plump Howdy Doody, it seemed he'd live forever. But we were burying him now, and the thud of his casket at the bottom of his grave had a very final ring to it.

I pulled up the collar of my overcoat. It had started to snow—large, wet flakes that stung as they hit and left Navoe Cemetery a pinto brown and white. Turning away from the wind and the snow and burying my head a little deeper in my coat, I remembered it was April, April Fools' Day, the most appropriate day I knew of to bury Si Buckles.

Si had never grown up. He had a childlike sense of humor, a child's penchant for practical jokes, and unfortunately a child's simple-minded cruelty. He'd been threatened more than once by more than one of us in Oakalla, but he was so much like a child it was hard to hate Si, even when he was pouring salt into your iced tea. Though I couldn't say I really knew him. I knew where he lived, where he worked, and that he wore the same plaid flannel shirt every day of his life. But he was like a fire siren— someone you never noticed until he rang in your ear. That bothered me. It seemed I'd buried too many like Si, that someone's life was somehow worth more than a one-paragraph obituary in my newspaper.

"Heart attack!" I heard someone say. "Came home from a poker game and dropped dead in his doorway."

"You're all wet!" his friend argued. "Bleeding ulcer. And Doc Baldwin had him nearly to the hospital before he died. Ain't that right, Doc?"

Dr. Fran Baldwin was a hard man to know, but an easy man to like. Slender and fair with a quick mind and a ready smile, he was good at everything he tried. And he never seemed to try too hard. Success came as naturally to him as the glow of his golden hair, and he wore it well, like a mantle the gods had decreed at birth. His easygoing charm was part of his attraction for a plodder like me. That and our shared love of the North Woods. Five summers before we'd guided a group of Boy Scouts through Quetico Provincial Park and discovered to our amazement that we made a great canoe team—he in the stern, I in the bow—and that led to other canoe trips and other outings in the wilderness. Then one frosty night along the Flambeau River we talked our campfire cold about the things that most mattered to us. The next day I helped him land the muskie that now hung on the wall of his den. After that we were friends.

But like the tortoise and the hare, we didn't always travel at the same speed and sometimes found ourselves uncomfortable in the other's shadow. Today was one of those days.

"You're both right," he said to those in question. "He died from a heart attack, but we got him as far as the hospital." He'd started walking, "Now, if you'll excuse me . . ."

"Sure thing, Doc."

He stopped when he saw me. "I see your eyes are dry, Garth," he said. He turned toward Si Buckles' grave. "But Si never had too many friends . . . and fewer mourners

I'd imagine." He turned back to me. "What brings you here? Idle curiosity or just being sociable?"

"A little of both."

"And then there's Diana, right?" He was smiling, but not with his usual flair. Nodding to an acquaintance, he moved on before I could answer.

It was snowing harder now. I noticed most of the others had already left. I didn't blame them. Navoe Cemetery was five miles from town, and the last two miles were gravel. The oldest cemetery in the county, it was seldom used anymore, and most of the stones still standing were nameless, their faces eroded like well-traveled coins. Desolation. That was Navoe. The road ended here, and on a day like this, grey and cold and damp, it sometimes seemed the world did, too.

And then there was Broken Claw, which sat in the first hollow west toward town. Broken Claw was a high, narrow, iron bridge with a ribbed top and a wooden floor that sagged and grumbled every time you drove over it. It'd been condemned for thirty years, and for thirty years they'd been saying it couldn't last another year—but it had—and many of those who prophesied its fall were now themselves buried in Navoe Cemetery.

Broken Claw. Its legend was as old as the bridge itself. When building the floor, a young Irishman named Tom O'Terrel slipped while carrying a timber, fell against a rock, and severed his index finger. It was not a major catastrophe—not in 1921 when there were a lot of Stubbies and Stumpies and Gimpies hobbling around— and those were the lucky ones. But it seemed like it to young Tom.

For he had a fair country fastball and a major-league curve and a dream of turning the newly dubbed Chicago Black Sox into the White Sox of old. But it's hard to throw a major-league curve when missing the index finger of your pitching hand. And it was hard for young Tom to cope with lost fame and fortune—especially after his little girl toddled in front of a bakery truck and his wife left him for parts unknown. He brooded for five years, drowning his troubles every night at the Shamrock Tavern (now the Corner Bar and Grill). Then one fine spring day (May 15, 1926—the small granite stone in Navoe reads) he jumped off Broken Claw and drowned himself.

As the story goes, on the night of a full moon you can see the silhouette of what appears to be a hand reaching out of the waters of Hog Run. The hand is very long and slender, almost monkeylike, and the index finger is missing. Hence the name, Broken Claw. But as all such stories go, only the true believers had seen the hand. I wasn't among them.

"Garth, are you coming by later?" I turned around to see her smiling at me. Her hair was light brown, almost blond, and her eyes were light grey, almost blue. Almost a blue-eyed blond, she stood five-four in her bare feet and came just to my chin. She was Diana Baldwin, the wife of Dr. Fran Baldwin.

"If I don't get stuck out here."

"Why don't you ride back with me?"

I nodded toward the brown Chevy sedan that once belonged to my grandmother. "If Jezebel spent the night out here, I wouldn't get her started again until July."

She gave me the sideways glance that meant she didn't agree with me, but if I wanted to be stupid, that was my right. "Then you'd better get started now."

"In a minute."

She glanced at the sky, next at me, then shook her head in amazement. "And you say I'm stubborn."

I watched her leave, her stride smooth and level like the draw of a gunfighter. She got in her car, a yellow Bentley she'd waxed until it glowed in the dark, and adjusted the rear-view mirror. She knew I was looking at her. She just wanted to make sure. I waved, and she waved, then drove away. I caught myself watching her for longer than was prudent. In the five years I'd known her we'd become the best of friends. She was easy to talk to, easy to listen to, and had an irritating grasp of the realities that sometimes eluded me. Not surprisingly, we argued a lot, joked a lot, kidded each other at every opportunity. All in good fun it once seemed. Now I wasn't so sure. Something in her eyes said it wasn't a game anymore; something inside me said the same thing. Evidently by his remark today Fran had noticed it, too. "And then there's Diana, right?" Right, Fran! Then there's Diana.

I glanced around the cemetery. Three of us were left: Phil Chesterson, Diana's older brother and Oakalla's only mortician, Fran Baldwin, and I. I turned and walked to my grandmother's grave. Kneeling, I brushed the snow from her name. Anna Marie Ryland. She'd raised four children by herself and helped put them all through college on butter-and-egg money. She'd left me a gunnysackful of advice, the small farm where she was raised, and Jezebel. She said that somehow, someday she'd bring me home to Oakalla, and she had with her death five years before. I was now overseer of her farm and the owner of the *Oakalla Reporter.* I also wrote a syndicated column that appeared weekly in about thirty local newspapers, including my own.

"Afternoon, Mr. Ryland."

"Afternoon, Ruben," I said, not looking up. I was never ready for Ruben Coalman, even when I knew he was coming. Tall, gaunt, and pale, he had the look of death warmed over. Twice. Warmed over twice in a black cauldron. And he always smiled. It wasn't a smile really, but a fixture, like the painted face of a circus clown, and it stayed with me long after Ruben had gone.

"I've been looking after your grandmother for you."

"I know you have, Ruben. I appreciate it."

Ruben was the guardian of Navoe Cemetery. He mowed it with a scythe, pulled the weeds around the stones, and kept out vandals. No one ever paid him for it. He earned what money he made with odd jobs in town. He owned little but his scythe and the clothes he wore. Even his ramshackle cabin was on someone else's property, a section of wooded creek bank only a river rat could love.

"Who are they burying today?" he asked.

"Si Buckles."

"Way out here?"

"They say it was his last request—to be buried in Navoe."

He peered through the driving snow. "Then that's Phil Chesterson and Fran Baldwin standing there." It was a natural association. Phil, Fran, and Si had grown up in Oakalla together and were lifelong friends and fellow pranksters. What one didn't think of, the other two did, though Phil and Fran's brand of humor was usually more subtle and often crueller than that of Si. Si would get you up in the dead of a winter night to answer a false fire alarm. Phil and Fran would go on to short sheet you, then put a boa constrictor in your bed while you were away.

Poor Si. He never seemed to realize when he was being used, and more often than not the joke he thought he was playing on someone else would end up being on him. Still he idolized Fran and trotted after him like a faithful setter, needing only an occasional pat on the head for all his trouble. If there was such a thing as a perfect stooge, Si Buckles was the perfect stooge.

"You know them, don't you, Mr. Ryland?" Ruben continued. "They're real funny guys."

"Yeah, I know them, Ruben." Fran and Phil took a long look our way before climbing into the hearse. "I'd better go, too." Ruben was starting to wear on me.

"You like it here, don't you, Mr. Ryland?"

I looked at him. He was still smiling, and his green eyes were calm and clear, like volcanic pools. It seemed I could see all the way to the bottom of his thoughts. "Why do you ask, Ruben?"

"I've seen you here before. You always take the time to

walk around . . . like you have real feelings for the dead."

I watched the snow fill in the tracks I'd made earlier. "It's a good place to think. No one ever bothers me here."

"Me either, Mr. Ryland. Most of the time I have the whole place to myself." He continued to gaze at me. His eyes had a woman's softness, the softness of a mother nursing her first born. "You'd better get going, Mr. Ryland, before you get stuck out here with me."

I didn't know whether it was the way he said it or the way I took it, but it was the loneliest sentence I'd ever heard a man speak.

I left Ruben standing in Navoe and walked to my car. Aptly named, Jessie, as I called her, had a long sorry history of betrayal at crucial times, and I'd never had the heart to drive her over a cliff, and I'd never had the guts to sell her to someone else. So, here we were together in the snow in Navoe Cemetery. I slowly let out the clutch and eased down the accelerator. Humor the old girl. It might work. It never had before, but it didn't hurt to try. She balked halfway up the first rise. I couldn't go forward, and I'd be damned if I'd back up and lose whatever ground I'd made, so I jammed her accelerator down, while her tires smoked and the snow and gravel flew. Then I was moving again. Glancing in the rear-view mirror, I saw Ruben pushing me. Soon I was over the top headed for Broken Claw, while he stopped in the middle of the road and waved until he was swallowed by the snow.

I plowed my way home, left Jessie in the driveway, and floundered to my back stoop, where I stomped my welcome mat, trying to feel my toes again. Ruth Krammes, my housekeeper, met me at the door. A big, raw-boned Swede with grey-blond hair, an imperious frown, and a heart of ten-karat gold, she had a Viking's thirst for life and two preferences among people. She either liked you or she didn't. I didn't know which was the greater curse. "I thought you said it wasn't going to snow," she said triumphantly, helping me inside.

"By all rights it shouldn't be."

"I should have bet you when I had the chance." It was a thing between us. We'd bet on anything—weather, sports, politics, grasshopper races. Once we even bet on a taffy pull. "My big toe said it was going to snow." She was staring me down, "And my big toe never lies." She took my coat and shook it. "You've got a hot bath waiting."

"Ruth, you're too good to me."

"Don't I know it."

After a long, hot bath had soaked the chill away, I dressed, then sat at the kitchen table and unfolded Friday's edition of the *Oakalla Reporter*. It wasn't one of my best efforts. But then again it wasn't my worst either. As Ruth put it, I was known for my "blazing mediocrity."

"Did you get him buried?" she asked.

I nodded, not looking up from the paper.

"Good riddance," she added.

I laid the paper down. "I thought he was your nephew?" I said. With Ruth, blood was always thicker than water. Except in my case. I figured I ranked somewhere among her third cousins, even though she claimed that was too high.

"He was my sister's boy. If that makes him my nephew, then I guess he was." She set a bowl of homemade vegetable soup in front of me. "But I can't be blamed for my sister's mistakes."

"Some people liked him."

"I can't be blamed for theirs either."

"Let me start all over."

"Please do."

"*What* didn't you like about him?"

"Everything. Would you like crackers?"

"Yes."

"Cheese?"

"Yes. Do you want to elaborate?"

"Don't talk with your mouth full." She blew on her soup to cool it. "Si buckles was a fool. He didn't just do anything for a joke. He *was* a joke. Once, he was a young joke. He grew into an old joke. Nothing's worse than an old joke. End of elaboration."

"I'm thinking about doing a feature on him."

That took her by surprise. She almost choked on her soup. "You're thinking about doing, *what?*"

"A feature. For my syndicated column."

"Why for God's sake? They're bad enough as it is."

"Why not? I for one would be interested in knowing the real Si Buckles. Who was he anyway? What were his hobbies, his interests, his most personal thoughts, if he had any? A man's life should amount to something, shouldn't it?"

"What do you mean by that?"

"I'm not sure what I mean. Except Si's dead, and nobody seems to give a damn. We all stood there dry eyed while we dropped him into his grave. That seems barbaric some- how, that no matter what his final judgment, he deserved at least one mourner."

"And that should have been me, right? Seeing I'm his nearest living relative?"

"No, Ruth. It's just a question for the ages. I'm not pointing a finger at anyone."

She dipped a spoonful of soup, blew on it to cool it, then dumped it back into the bowl. "Uncle Charlie again?"

"May be." Hail fellow well met, that was my Uncle Charlie. A salesman all his life, he had a suitcaseful of stories and a laugh that would fill a ballroom. He was my favorite uncle from the time he first bounced me on his knee until the night I closed his eyes in death. December 23. I remembered because they were singing Christmas carols outside his door. I went to the window, looked out at the December snow, and tried to cry. For me mainly, because at thirty-nine I wasn't yet ready for the changing of the guard, to fill Uncle Charlie's shoes. Couldn't cry. Went outside and walked and walked and walked.

"Are you feeling a little lonely, is that it? A little like Uncle Charlie?"

"A lot like Uncle Charlie. That's the most I can ever hope to be, somebody's uncle."

She shrugged. She'd had two children, lost both of them. A daughter to polio, a son to war. "Welcome to the club."

I put some crackers in my soup. I wanted to change the subject. "Ruben Coalman, how old is he?"

"Somewhere around forty. Why do you ask?"

"He seems younger. Has he always been like that?"

She fluffed like a mother hen defending one of her brood. "Like what?"

"Distant. Like neither one of us is really there."

"You mean crazy?"

"No, I don't mean crazy. Like he's in a world all his own."

"You mean crazy."

"Okay. I mean crazy."

"He's *not* crazy."

"Forget it. Pass the cheese, please."

"All right, he's crazy. But not the way most people think. He's a gentle crazy. He doesn't need to be locked up."

"I didn't say he did. I asked how long he'd been that way."

"Since he was seventeen."

"What happened then?"

"Nobody knows. He just snapped one night."

"Just like that?" I snapped my fingers.

"Just like that. He used to come to my house every Sunday, and we'd go over his vocabulary words for school together. One Sunday he was fine, and the next he came in with that silly smile and that nothing in his eyes that's been there ever since. He didn't even know why he was there. He must've come out of habit."

"What was he like before?"

"Smart as a whip. A little nervous and tongue-tied when he had to get up in front of people, but he had a mind like a steel trap. Once something went in, it never came out. He wanted to be a veterinarian. He'd have made a good one, too." She was mulling a thought. "You're not thinking of doing a feature on Ruben?"

"No. I was just curious. What about his parents?"

"What about them?"

"Did he have any, or was he dropped out of a dirigible on his head in the middle of Navoe?"

She scowled at me. I could feel myself wither. "His father died when he was a baby, his mother when he was sixteen. He's looked after himself ever since. Any more questions?"

"When did he move to Navoe?"

"I don't know. Maybe after his mother died." She studied me. "You're dressed again."

"Shouldn't I be?"

"That means you're going out again."

"I'm old enough."

She dipped her spoon into her soup, but brought it out empty. "Where are you going, in case I have to send a wrecker?"

"Fran Baldwin's, and I'm walking."

"Hmph!" she snorted. "Hmph!" Their feud went a long way back. She was one of the few people who didn't like Dr. Fran Baldwin. I'd asked her once why and was told to mind my own business. "For the life of me, I don't see what you find to like in that man . . ." Her brows rose, "Unless it's Diana?"

"We're friends, that's all."

"I've heard that one before."

"On my honor."

She laughed. She knew I didn't have any.

It was still snowing when I left, soft mounds piling in the street like whipped-cream topping. Two days before I'd caught my first real breath of spring. Trudging through the snow, the wind pressed to my throat, I tried to recall the sensation. I didn't have much luck.

Fran and Diana Baldwin lived in a two-story brick house near the heart of town. Though its corner lot was the largest in Oakalla, it wasn't an expensive house. It was a century-old farmhouse—square and solid and comfortable with thick walls and hardwood floors and the feel of home. Diana took my coat and led me into the family room. Papered blue and white, with a walnut railing around the top to hold Diana's antique plates, and a brick fireplace that entirely covered one wall, the family room was my favorite place to sit. I found it very easy to enter, very hard to leave. "Fran, Garth's here."

Fran stood, shook my hand, and poured me a Scotch on the rocks. "Well, what shall we toast tonight?" he asked, as he handed me my Scotch. "Si Buckles, our dear departed friend. . . . or my wife, and her newest declaration of independence?"

"Fran, now's not the time." Diana's voice had an edge to it.

I'd come at the wrong time. The tension was as thick as the smoke rolling up the chimney. I walked to the fireplace, took a log from the copper boiler they used as a woodbox, and threw it on top of the others. That's all it needed, as a bright yellow flame shot up and spread its warmth across the room. Out of all those who owned fireplaces, maybe one out of ten knew enough about wood and enough about draft and enough about kindling to lay a good fire. Fran was the one out of ten. Something else must be on his mind tonight. I looked up. The fire was working its magic, as the tension began to melt. "You make a good drink," I said to Fran.

"Yes, you do," Diana said, "and I'd like another." He took her glass from her and walked to the kitchen, as Diana sat beside me and lightly touched my hand. "Thank you. We've been at each other all evening."

"Life's too short for that."

"That's what I keep telling myself . . . among other things."

"Do you want to talk about it?"

"Maybe later."

Fran returned with her drink, but stopped a few feet away, his shadow draped like a black flag across us. Then I noticed Diana's hand still rested against mine. Diana noticed at the same time and casually withdrew it to her lap. "So what have you been doing with yourself lately?" she asked.

"Which one of us do you mean?" Fran answered, sitting on the other side of her.

She laughed. "I'll start with Garth."

"Nothing lately. Right now I'm looking for this week's feature."

Fran smiled, "Why not do one on Si Buckles?"

"I'm thinking about it."

"Garth, you can't mean it!" Diana said. "Anybody but him."

"What's wrong with Si Buckles?" I asked.

Fran rose and walked to the window, watching the snow. He did seem preoccupied, that his thoughts were somewhere else. "You'll have to excuse Diana. Si wasn't a favorite of hers."

"Then you tell me who'd want to read about a man who wore the same green shirt every day of his adult life?" Diana asked.

"Maybe the shirtmaker," Fran laughed. "It must be some kind of record." I liked his laugh. It had a defiant ring to it. It was the laugh of a gypsy or a freedom fighter or anyone else who put life above all. "Actually, it wasn't the same shirt. They changed over the years, even day to day. In fact, I saw him in a suit once. It wasn't the shirt, but the color green he loved, especially when it came in plaids." He still watched the snow, as it swooped by the window. "Of course, Diana's never approved of any of my friends . . . except you, Garth. And I'm not sure whether

I chose you or she did. No matter. It's all in the family." He studied me. "But tell me, if you had a wife as beautiful as Diana, would you trust her out of your sight?"

"No, I don't think so." I felt Diana's elbow dig into my ribs. "I'd probably lock her in her room every day."

The phone rang. Fran moved quickly to answer it, as though he'd been expecting it. "Yes, I know it's still snowing," he said. "What do you want me to do about it?" He sighed. "Okay, I'll be right over." He hung up and stared out the window at the driving snow.

"What's wrong?" Diana asked.

"Emergency."

"Anyone I know?"

He shook his head and walked from the room. A few minutes later I heard the front door open and close.

"What was that all about?" I asked Diana.

"I don't know. You never know with Fran."

"He didn't try to take the car," I observed. "Is there anyone in Oakalla you don't know?"

"There didn't used to be. I don't get out as much as I once did. Why the questions?"

"It's my nose acting up. It does every time I smell a story."

"He's probably gone over to Phil's. He'll get a ride from there wherever he's going." She hadn't offered to move, and it was warm where she was touching me. "You can follow him if you like."

"No, I'll pass."

"Then I'll go get something I've been wanting to show you."

I added two more logs to the fire, but I didn't like the way they sat. Using the poker, I wallowed them around until I was satisfied. I looked up. Diana was laughing at me. She had a roguish laugh. It was almost evil. "It has to be right," I said, "or it won't burn."

"Did I say anything?"

"What do you have behind your back?"

She held it in front of her for me to see. It was a portrait of Ruben Coalman. "What do you think?" she asked.

I was held by his eyes, his smile that seemed to turn inward to mock his soul. It wasn't the Ruben Coalman I knew. She'd added another dimension, one I couldn't define, but whether the perception was hers or his, it was frightening to behold. "I think it's your best."

"So do I." She handed it to me. "He has an arresting face, don't you think?"

"Yes. It's almost spooky." I handed it back to her, glad to be rid of it. "How do you happen to know Ruben?"

"We went to school together. He was in Fran's class."

"Do you know what happened to him, why he lost his mind?"

Her eyes were suddenly opaque, as if she'd pulled the shutters down. "No. I don't think anyone does. I've sort of looked after him lately—finding him odd jobs to do around town and giving him money when he needed it." She stroked the portrait, reluctant to let it go. "He's a very lonely man. I wish somehow I could reach him."

I gazed at the portrait. "I think you have." It wasn't what I was thinking, but it was what came out.

She set the portrait aside. "You build a nice fire."

"Thank you."

"May I fix you anything?"

"No. I'm fine."

"Like your back rubbed?" She pressed her thumbs to my shoulders and began to gently massage them. Some women have iron in their hands, others cotton. Hers were more like separate beams of sunlight, and I could feel my heartbeat in her palms. "You weren't much help tonight," she said.

"Doing what?"

"Getting me a job."

"I was just kidding."

"Fran wasn't. That's what we were arguing about before you came. He doesn't want me working."

"Why?"

"You'll have to ask him."

"Why do you want to go to work?"

"I'm tired of being kept."

"Reason enough. What do you want to do?"

"I'd like to paint. I feel about eight feet tall whenever I finish a portrait. But there's no money in it."

"Is money that important?"

"It is if you've never earned any. It buys your self-respect." Her hand swept the room. "You see those plates up there? They're R. S. Prussia. That vase is satin glass, and that pitcher is holly amber. I drive a Bentley, wear tailor-made imports, and have been known, on one occasion in New Orleans, to eat a hundred-dollar breakfast. And do you know what I did to earn all that? I learned how to dress, make myself up, and to say no until the right man came along. That's right. Fran was my first. Virgins bring a premium, you know. They always have for some strange reason known only to God and men. Of course, I'm college educated and well bred as far as Oakalla goes. Not the best blood line, the Baldwins are the best, but perhaps the top ten. I read my book a week and play my bridge on Wednesday and buy Girl Scout cookies every year. I sometimes sleep with my husband and sometimes enjoy it, and occasionally, when I have the courage, I look at myself in the mirror—mornings are best, before make-up—and see a thirty-seven-year-old woman who hasn't done a damn thing with her life."

"Don't you think you're being a little hard on yourself?"

"No. Not at all. I'm being honest with myself for the first time. My dream was a bummer, Garth. I don't like being Mrs. America."

"I've never had that problem."

"That's because you're a man."

"That's because I'm poor. The places I eat don't have a hundred-dollar menu, let alone a hundred-dollar break-fast. I couldn't eat it if they did." I got up and walked to the window. The snow had stopped, and the moon momentarily peeped through, washing its yellow light across the lawn.

"Come back here," she said softly. When I didn't, she joined me at the window, her arms slowly encircling me. "Okay, what's wrong?" she asked. "Your back has rocks in it."

"Nothing's wrong. My back always has rocks in it. It's an occupational hazard." I didn't tell her my back had rocks in it because my head had rocks in it. I should never let myself be alone with her—not at night, not with a fire in the fireplace and Scotch under my belt. It was the worst kind of torture, and I wasn't that strong.

"Is it because I'm married?"

"That has crossed my mind."

"Most men would find that more than convenient. You dine as often as you like, whenever you like, and someone else picks up the tab."

"I'm not most men. When I was married, I never cheated on my wife, though God knows I wanted to. Call it hypocrisy if you want, but as long as she was wearing my ring, I thought I owed her that much."

"And do you think I owe Fran that much?"

"Yes, I think you do. Now I'd better go."

"Whatever you say." She got my coat and walked me to the door. "Thanks for coming." Her voice was cool, controlled, just husky enough to betray her disappointment in me.

I traced her sleeve from her wrist to her shoulder. Her silk dressing gown was cool to touch. My hand stopped against her face. Her cheek had the same coolness. "I'm sorry, Diana."

"What's there to be sorry about? I made an offer. You refused it. We're still friends, aren't we?"

I lightly kissed her. She didn't respond. "Still friends."

I stepped outside, as a gust of wind peppered me with snow, and walked home. Wedged in the storm door just above the handle was what looked like part of a grocery sack. Probably a note from Ruth, telling me to take off my boots before I tracked up the house. But it wasn't Ruth's writing. The words were scrawled, barely legible. It read simply: "Si Buckles lives." That was good to know. Especially when I was looking forward to a long winter's nap.

C H A P T E R   2

It seemed I'd just hit the bed and rolled over when the phone rang. I stumbled down the stairs and answered it.

"Garth?"

"Yes, Rupert?"

"Got a break-in at the hardware. You interested?"

I yawned. "Not particularly. But I'll meet you there in a few minutes."

I hung up as Ruth brushed past me on her way down the stairs. "You'll eat something first," she said.

"Just burn me a piece of toast."

"That won't last as far as the door."

"Then burn me two pieces of toast."

"I'll burn you a mushroom omelet."

It was hard to argue with that.

Outside, the main streets were already plowed, as Oakalla was alive with garden tractors and snow blowers. I didn't own either. I had a snow shovel somewhere that I hadn't seen since February. I accused Ruth of hiding it, and she accused me, but neither one of us had looked very hard for it. Today, though, I didn't need it. My neighbor had plowed my drive. I made a mental note to have a case of Leinenkugel's sitting on his porch before sundown.

Sheriff Rupert Roberts stood in front of the hardware, blowing on his hands to warm them. He was tall and thin with stoop shoulders and bloodhound eyes and the look of a man unjustly persecuted all of his life. We had an agreement. He'd call me whenever he thought I'd be interested, and I'd mention his name in my paper whenever possible, especially during election year. "Morning, Garth." He never did anything in a hurry, and when he spoke, it seemed his words were a half count behind his mouth.

"Morning, Rupert. What do you have here?"

"I'm not exactly sure." He reached through a broken pane and unlatched the hardware door. "It looks like a broken window."

"I see it does."

He reached into his pocket, pulled out his tobacco pouch, and took a chew. "Want some?"

"No, thanks."

"It's good for what ails you."

"I swallowed some once. I haven't chewed it since."

"I guess that would put fire in your ears." He spit into the snow. "Nice day . . . for January. Though, don't get me wrong. I like it. I was telling Elvira this morning how much I like to get out in the dark and the cold and the snow. Especially in April. Especially for a broken window. Especially when I just got to bed."

"That's all, a broken window?"

"Near as Fritz and I can tell. We've both been over the hardware backwards and forward, and we can't find nothing missing."

"When did Fritz find the broken window?"

"This morning when he opened up."

"Was the door locked?"

"He said it was."

"Mind if I look?"

"Be my guest." He threw open the door.

I entered the hardware. "What were you doing up all night?" I knew when I asked that I shouldn't have.

"Well, you did know it snowed? And it seems to me whenever it snows people would naturally want to be inside . . . by a fire . . . a big bowl of buttered popcorn and a cold beer in front of them . . ." He shook his head. "No. As soon as it snows, some fool's got to get out in it. Then that's *so* much fun, he's got to get his family out in it. Then his neighbors, then his friends, then his enemies . . . Well, most of them, some way or other manage to get back home. Some don't." He picked up a phone book. "Does it look like to you I've got a phosphorescent phone number?"

"No."

"I must have. Because it's the only number they can find at night. By the time I was through pushing and pulling and stomping and cussing I had maybe an hour's sleep left. I'd just closed my eyes when *dingaling!* It was Tillie, Tillie Mertz. This time she had some graverobbers cornered in Navoe Cemetery. I deputized her over the phone and told her to get her shotgun and go after them. She said she must have been mistaken and hung up." He spit on the floor. "Between her and Ruben I think Navoe has the corner on crazies." We were now at the back of the hardware. "If Tillie doesn't call me at least once a week," he said, "I know something's wrong with her. Last week aliens were crawling down her chimney. She pointed her shotgun and cut loose. Cleaned out her damper, her flue, and a raccoon all at the same time."

"I'm glad it wasn't Christmas Eve."

"That would be kind of hard to explain to your kids, wouldn't it?" He looked around the store. "See anything we missed?"

"No."

"I still can't figure how the window got broken."

"It could've been the wind."

"Could have. That's about all I can come up with." We walked outside. "Can I buy you breakfast?"

"No. I've eaten."

"How about a cup of coffee?"

"No. I've got somewhere else I need to go."

"Where's that?"

"Si Buckles'."

"What's there?"

"I don't know yet. Maybe nothing. I'm thinking about doing a feature on him."

"That'd be my second choice."

"What's your first?"

"My cat had kittens yesterday."

"What's wrong with Si Buckles?"

"Nothing his death didn't cure." He put his hand on my shoulder for silence. *"Listen.* What *is* that?"

"A robin."

"What's he got to sing about?" He spit in the snow. "Si Buckles, huh? I think I'll cancel my subscription."

Si Buckles lived in a small white frame house at the north edge of town. His lot was part of the subdivision that had claimed the pasture where I once played baseball as a kid. All the houses in the subdivision had the same cynical twenty-year-old look, like that of career soldiers who knew their best years were behind them. There were a couple spindly elms in Si's front yard, an evergreen that needed trimming beneath his frosted bathroom window, and, couched beside the sidewalk with its bristles up, a winter-killed rose bush that I remembered as once having the reddest roses in town. I was surprised to see footprints in the snow. I wasn't Si's first caller this morning.

I took the piece of grocery sack from my pocket and reread it. The message was clear: "Si Buckles lives." The question was, who wrote it and why?

Was it Fran and Phil back to their old tricks? Possibly. They had ample opportunity last night. But I didn't think so. The tone was all wrong for them. There was nothing lighthearted in this message, no crinkle of laughter around the edges. Heavy. That's the way I'd felt since I'd first put it in my pocket this morning. Though I couldn't say why. Maybe it was the paper on which it was written—

Kroger brown. Or maybe it was the message itself. "Si Buckles lives." What the hell did he mean by that?

I went inside. Si kept a neat house, neater than I expected, but there were wet smudges on the kitchen linoleum where someone had been walking recently, and the faint smell of cigarette smoke hung in the air. I wondered who'd been here. Maybe the gas man taking a final reading? No. It couldn't be. The meter was outside.

I followed the smudges to Si's bedroom and opened the east curtain to let some light in and help clear out the threads of smoke still hanging. The sun was up, and the trees were starting to shed the snow like clumps of wet fur. The sun felt good, better than the musty chill of Si's bedroom. I turned back to the room and saw that his clothes closet was open. Inside, all in a row, were several green plaid flannel shirts along with several pairs of green work pants. Fran was right. It was the color green Si loved, especially when it came in plaid.

I looked for books. He didn't own any. I looked for hobbies. He didn't have any. I looked for photographs. There weren't any. I checked the small portable television beside his bed. It wasn't working. Judging by its condition, it hadn't worked for some time.

Opening the top drawer of his chest, I saw that it was scrambled, his socks piled at one end as if they'd been dumped there. The other drawers looked the same way. Either Si had palsy, or somebody had been rummaging through them. I stepped backwards and felt my shoe scrape something hard on the floor. I picked it up. It was a key, long and thin like the kind to a lockbox, but there was no number on it. I wondered what it went to and what it was doing in the middle of the floor.

I searched under the bed, then the closet, where digging through a pile of soiled clothes, I found a battered metal chest. I tried the key. The lock was rusty, but I finally made the key work. I dragged the chest into the sunlight, opened it, and glanced inside at what looked like stacks of old notebooks. I picked up the one on top, turned to the last entry, and began to read: "Another day. Gee, I wish Doc or Phil would come by. It sure gets lonely without those two. Just one more day! Just one more day! I can't wait!" I set the notebook down. Evidently Si kept a diary and had for some time. I reread his last entry. I closed my eyes and shook my head. His weekly poker game coming up, and he was in rapture. As I glanced around his bedroom, it seemed even smaller than before.

I picked up the diary to put it back. Wednesday. His last entry was on Wednesday. I wondered what had happened to Thursday's entry. Then I saw it was missing, the page neatly torn out without leaving a raveling behind.

Someone charged into the house, slamming the door on his way in. Only one person I knew entered a house like that—Phil Chesterson, Diana's older brother. He had a square build, a square jaw, a blond flattop, and looked like the Marine sergeant he once was. He owned the mortuary, but was as suited for the profession as I was for steeple-jack. Not that he couldn't prepare a body for showing. Technically he was as good as they came. But his deathside manner lacked the finesse one usually needs at such times. Not the heart, though. He could cry with the best of them and usually did, causing me to wonder why he hadn't cried for his old friend Si Buckles.

"What the hell are you doing here?" he asked when he saw me sitting on the floor.

"I might ask you the same thing?"

"Does Doc know you're here?"

To Phil, Fran was and always had been Doc. They seemed more like brothers than friends, that as the favored son, Fran carried the family colors, and there was nothing better for Phil to do than tag along and hope some of Fran's aura rubbed off. It was sad in a way. It seemed to put a burden on both of them.

"I don't need his blessing, nor yours, for that matter." I

tried to lift the chest of diaries. I couldn't without risking a double hernia. "Now why don't you help me with this?"

He thought a moment. He'd been burned once too many times by snap decisions. And in all probability would be again. "Okay. Where do you want it?"

"In the trunk of my car. It'll take both of us."

He lifted it easily. "I don't think so."

Once outside, the chest resting securely in Jessie's trunk, Phil lighted a cigarette and leaned against a tree. "Sorry to barge in on you. Doc asked me to keep a close eye on the place."

"No harm, no foul," I said.

"I was here earlier," he offered. "Somebody had jim-mied the door to get in. That's why I came back."

"Did you see who it was?"

"No. I heard the back door slam when I came in the front. I ran to the window, but he was gone. That's when I saw the fresh tracks leading away from the house and back into town. I tried to follow them, but didn't have much luck. They ended right in the middle of Fair Haven Road."

"Maybe he caught a ride with somebody?"

"That's what it looked like. Unless he spread his wings and flew?" He looked to me to confirm it.

"Maybe he did." I didn't want to disappoint him. Besides, I was ready to leave.

He was staring at Jessie's trunk. He had an anxious smile on his face, like he'd just been caught with his hand in the cookie jar. "You mind telling me what's in there?"

"In where?"

"That metal chest I carried out."

"Diaries. Or to be more specific, Si Buckles' diaries."

"Diaries! What the hell do you mean by *diaries?*" He threw his cigarette down and looked hard at Jessie's trunk, like he wanted to tear it open with his bare hands. "Jesus Christ!"

I reached into my pocket for my keys, prepared to throw them if worse came to worse. "What's the problem?"

But he didn't answer. He took one threatening step toward me, changed his mind as he spun on his heels and ran for his truck. The last I saw of him, he was barreling down Fair Haven Road into town.

I got in Jessie and drove toward home. I met Ruben Coalman coming toward me with a feed sack slung over his shoulder. I stopped and rolled down my window. "Would you like a lift?" I asked.

"No, Mr. Ryland, I'll manage." It was always Mr. Ryland, never Garth. I sometimes felt like his grandfather.

"You walk all the way from home?"

"Sure, I do every day."

"What about the snow?"

He glanced around, a bewildered look on his face.

"Didn't it slow you down?"

"It might have. I didn't pay much attention." His smile seemed broader than usual, almost conscious.

"What's in the sack?" I asked.

"Cracked corn . . . for the birds. They've come north expecting spring. They're not ready for snow."

"I'm with them." I noticed his worn leather jacket and threadbare pants. "Aren't you cold, Ruben?"

"Not if I keep moving."

"Then I'd better let you go."

"I don't mind, Mr. Ryland. It's not often I have a chance to talk to someone."

"You sure I can't take you somewhere?"

"I'm sure."

I drove home. Ruth held the door open for me, as I dragged the metal chest inside and up the stairs to my study.

"What's in there?" she asked, eyeing it suspiciously.

"Fan mail."

"That chest looks familiar."

"It should. It belonged to Si Buckles."

She set her jaw. "It belonged to me! I wondered where it got to! Where'd you find it?"

"His closet. Right next to his shoes, I believe."

"What's really in it?"

"Diaries."

"Whose?"

"Whose do you think? You can read them if you like. You might be remembered fondly."

"I'd sooner read a Kleenex box. What are *you* doing with them?"

"I don't know yet. Maybe I'll find my feature inside."

She studied me warily. "Level with me, Garth. What do you really have up your sleeve?"

"Nothing. I'm digging, that's all. Ninety-nine times out of a hundred I come up dry. I probably will this time, but I don't know that yet."

She shrugged. "I thought I'd ask."

I took a shot in the dark. It was more a hunch than anything else, that she knew something about Si Buckles that she wasn't telling me. "Ruth, are you holding out on me?"

She flushed. It seemed even her hair turned red. "I don't know what you're talking about."

I pointed my finger at her. "Guilty as charged!"

"With good reason. And that's all I'll say."

She went downstairs, as I stared at the metal chest. I was sorry I didn't have time today to go through it.

CHAPTER 3

The next morning at breakfast Ruth was mulling a thought, as she absent-mindedly stirred her coffee for the third time. "You ever see a cat swim?" she asked.

"No."

"He can. Not very well, but he can. You know why he doesn't?"

"For the same reason I don't. He doesn't like to."

"Right. You ever see a duck walk?"

"A few times."

"Can't very well, can he?"

"Not very well." I was sure there was a point to all of this.

"Which would you say walks better, a duck or a cat?"

"A cat."

"Swims better?"

"Duck."

"Climbs better?"

"Cat."

"Flies better?"

"Duck."

"Then they're even, right? They both can do what the other can't."

"Right."

"Then why do we always say he waddles like a duck, but never he swims like a cat?"

"I hope that didn't keep you up last night."

"No, I'm serious. The duck comes out on the short end every time. When did you last hear the story *The Ugly Cat?* Pass the bread, please."

"What brought all this on?"

"The butter, too." She pointed her knife at me and squinted. "I keep seeing all the 'beautiful people' plastered everywhere I look. It galls my soul, that's all."

"Why's that?"

"What did they do to earn it? Take Jackie what's-her-name. Where would she be if she looked like Eleanor Roosevelt?"

"Forest Lawn."

"You're not taking me seriously. You should because you're one of the ducks of the world." Fran Baldwin knocked on the back door. "And here comes one of the cats."

Ruth let him in and poured him coffee. Then she left, and I didn't see her again. I ate her bacon and gave her eggs to the neighbor's dog. Fran sat sipping his coffee. He seemed in no hurry, though I knew he had patients waiting. "I get the feeling she doesn't like me," he said.

"She probably has things to do."

"It was just an observation." He swirled the coffee around in his cup. "You still plan to do a story on Si?"

"If I can find one."

"Phil's worried. As you might know, we did a lot of rotten things in the past. We'd both prefer they'd stay forgotten."

I studied him. "What changed your mind?"

"What do you mean?"

"Sunday night you were all for doing a story on Si."

"Sunday night was Sunday night. Today is today. I'm sober now . . . in a lot of ways. I'm trying to play it straight from now on, and I don't think your story will help me any."

"I don't see how it'll hurt you."

"Have you read the diaries?"

"No."

"That's what I thought."

"I don't even know if I'm going to use them."

"You'll use them."

"How can you be so sure? What's in them anyway?"

"As I said, a lot of things I'd prefer to stay forgotten. I'm not just asking for myself. It's mainly for Phil. Whether he shows it or not, the war took its toll on him. It took him a long time to learn to like himself again, even longer to get his business to where he could break even. He can't afford a setback now. He'll never recover."

"Fran, you've lost me somewhere. One minute we're talking about doing a human-interest story on Si and the next I'm taking food out of the mouths of Phil's kids. Just how big a skeleton is there in your closet?"

"I said I wasn't asking for me. I'm asking for Phil."

"In his closet then?" I reached into my pocket and handed him the grocery-sack note I'd found in my door. "Does it have anything to do with this? Are you and Phil trying to work some angle on me?"

He read the note. To his credit he stayed reasonably calm, though his face was as white as Ruth's tablecloth. His hand closed tightly over the note. I was afraid I wouldn't get it back again. "Where did you get this?" he demanded.

"I found it in my back door. I don't have the slightest idea what it's about. Do you?"

He opened his hand and let the note drop on the table. "No."

"Then you didn't write it?"

"No. Neither did Phil if that's your next question."

"What do you make of it? Surely you have some idea."

The color had just now started to return to his face. "Some sick mind at work. That's about all I can say." He rose unsteadily. For a cat, he was suddenly heavy on his feet. "Sorry to bother you, Garth. I guess I wasted both our time."

"I'll think about what you said, Fran. But no promises, okay?"

His voice was mocking. "I guess I really don't deserve any." He gave me a half-hearted wave and left.

I retrieved the note and went upstairs to my study where the diaries were. I opened the chest and took one out. I hesitated. I didn't like its feel in my hand. And I didn't like the smell coming from the chest—it had the faint odor of decay, like a mouse had crawled in there and died. Maybe Si Buckles *should* stay buried. Maybe I was trespassing on unholy ground. But I wouldn't know until I read the diaries.

I began to read. An hour passed. I was barely aware of it. Another hour passed. I was still on the first diary. I heard someone on the stairs. "Ruth, is that you?"

"No, it's Diana."

"Come on up and have a seat."

She laid her coat on my desk and sat beside me on the floor. "What's that look on your face?" she asked.

I handed her a diary. "Read it."

Another hour passed. Diana was still on her first diary. She hadn't moved. I wasn't even sure she'd turned the page. Then she glanced my way, saw that I was watching, and put the diary down. Picking up another one, she began reading aloud: "'It's all set. Tonight we move. I can hardly wait for Old Harry Chase to finally get his. *I* get to pull the string this time. Fran promised. I start shaking every time I think about it. Tonight *I* get to pull the string!'" She looked up at me, her eyes wide in disbelief. "Garth, that's almost pathological. I knew he was odd. I didn't know he was sick."

"You should read what's in here. A month ago he tied two cats together by their tails and threw them over a clothesline. They clawed each other to death. But listen to this: 'Doc has just told me I have a year at most to live. It's a rare disease, and always fatal. It starts in the bone marrow and spreads throughout the body. That's why I've been so weak lately. Doc says the medicine will only help for a while. I don't mind. I've had my share of fun. I'd just like to have one last laugh sometime before I die. Doc and Phil keep promising me, but they've never told me what they're planning.' Okay, that was a month ago. Now, let me read his last entry: 'Another day. Gee, I wish Doc or Phil would come by. It sure gets lonely without those two. Just one more day! Just one more day! I can't wait!'" I set the diary down. "I thought he was talking about his weekly poker game. I'm not so sure now."

"You think it was something else he was waiting for?"

"It might've been." I didn't tell her about the page that had been torn out of the diary, the page that might have told me what it was.

"You think he got so excited he had a heart attack? That would be irony, wouldn't it? The last laugh was on him." She sat back, thumbing through another diary. "Fran and Phil don't come off very well in these, do they? They seem nearly as sick as he was—though with less reason. No wonder Fran was so upset when Phil told him about the diaries. He was here earlier this morning, wasn't he?"

"Yes. He asked me to go easy on him."

"And what did you say?"

"I told him I'd do what I could, but no promises."

"That seems fair enough."

"What about you? What do you think?"

"I know you well enough to know it doesn't matter what I think." She sat up, letting the diary slide from her hand. "It's more than frightening, isn't it, to see it all in black and white? I wonder how many of us will want to see the ledger when it's over. Not our pretense, nor our rhetoric, nor our dreams, but the bare details of our lives. I think that if there is a hell, that would truly be it. I know it would for me."

I lay back on the floor, staring at the ceiling. She had a point. Considering my life up to the present, I wasn't quite ready to cash in my chips. They wouldn't even buy me bus fare out of town. "They say life begins at forty."

"Thirty-seven."

"What?"

"I'm thirty-seven. You're forty. Don't make it any worse than it is."

"My apology."

"Accepted."

I picked up the first diary she'd been reading. "Did you find what you were looking for?"

"Who said I was looking for anything?"

"Your eyes, as you were reading."

"Were you spying on me?" She was avoiding my question. She was a master at that.

"You can't sit two feet away and not expect me to look at you."

She sat on my stomach, opening another diary. "And he shall not covet his neighbor's wife, nor his manservant, nor his maidservant . . ."

"Get off."

"Nor his gizzard, nor his ass . . ."

I sat up, toppling her into my arms. "You never answered my question. Did you find what you were looking for?"

She pulled me to her. Her sweater was soft—cashmere, and it felt good to touch. My hand found her breast and rested there. "Go ahead. You're allowed inside."

"Are you going to answer my question?"

She kicked the study door closed. "Maybe."

But she didn't. I set her on the floor and pulled away from her. I wasn't a game-player at heart, and this game was getting serious.

"What's wrong?" she asked.

"Nothing. It's just not the time, nor the place."

"I want you. You want me. What better time or place?"

"Don't expect me to answer that."

"What are you afraid of, that we'll hurt Fran? He'll never have to know."

"I'm the one I have to live with. And lately I haven't been sleeping very well the way it is."

"You don't sleep with married women, is that it?"

"As a rule, no. I like an open relationship. I like to be seen with my lady, know the door's always open if either one of us needs a friend. I don't mean the closet door either."

"What if I were to divorce Fran?"

"Are you really ready for that?"

"I don't know. Am I? You've been through a divorce. What's it like?"

What *was* it like? After seven years I should have some profound thoughts on the subject. But I didn't. Mostly watered-down memories that didn't begin to tell the true tale. "Vulnerable, lonely, bitter—even when you try your best not to let it be. A lot of entanglements you didn't know you had. A lot of words you wished you had back. A lot of mistakes getting back into love again. Not something I'd recommend. Only as a last resort."

"What makes you think divorce isn't my last resort?" Her face hardened, "Or would you rather I shot him?"

I didn't like the look in those grey eyes of hers. It told me she was capable of either. "I'd rather I took you home."

The snow was nearly gone except for a few patches in the deep shade. I let Diana off at home and turned onto Gas Line Road, which led east out of town toward Navoe Cemetery. The winter wheat was thick and green, and the willows, sprouting yellow buds, drooped like strawstacks along the road. Turning onto the gravel, I hit my first bug of the year.

Tillie Mertz lived with ten cats, four dogs, a pig, and a goat at the top of a small hill overlooking Navoe on one side and Broken Claw on the other. Her two-story log house had never been painted, and you could see through the chinks in its brick chimney, but it had stood for over a century that way, and likely would stand for a century more. Tillie and the pig and the goat were in the yard. She wore a bonnet, an apron, and an ankle-length dress, and she squinted as I approached, like she was drawing a bead on me. I was glad to see she was holding a rake and not a shotgun like the last time I saw her.

"Morning, Tillie," I said, as four hounds in full voice converged on me.

"It's afternoon." She put two fingers to her mouth, and with one shrill whistle that nearly took off the top of my head, sent the hounds scurrying back into the woods.

I glanced at the sun. "So it is."

"What you want?"

"Just visiting."

"It's a first, ain't it?"

"Second. The first time you ran me off."

"You should never come after sundown."

"You made that clear."

She began raking. "Well, visit."

I looked up at the sky. "Nice day."

"A little cool in the shade."

"You're right." I looked at the house. It leaned to the north. It seemed that any day it might slide down the hill into Navoe. "Lived here long?"

"I was born here, same as my mother. I intend to die here." She glanced up at me. "You plan to write that?"

"I might."

"Make it soon. I want to read it while I still can."

"I'll see what I can do." I looked across Navoe Cemetery. "Is that Ruben down there?"

"Who else?"

"What's he doing?"

"Probably pulling weeds. If you want to know why, you'll have to ask him."

"You known Ruben long?"

"All his life."

"You know what happened to him?"

"Nope. But I can guess."

"Why don't you guess?"

"What's the point? The harm's already done."

"You're probably right." I watched her pig stick its head through a hole in the screen door and look inside. "Sheriff Roberts said you had company out here early Monday morning."

"We did."

"What did you see?"

She leaned on her rake. "Graverobbers, just like I told Sheriff Roberts."

"How do you know they were graverobbers?"

"What else would they be doing at that hour?"

"I can think of several things."

She squinted at me. "Such as?"

"Well, maybe one thing."

"In a half-foot of snow? Which one of us is the crazy?"

"I hope not either one of us."

"You believe me then?"

"I believe someone might have been here. I still can't believe they were graverobbers. Did you recognize them?"

She shrugged. "Maybe I did. What's it to you?"

"I'm curious, that's all."

"Curiosity killed old tom."

"So I've heard."

She wiped her forehead with her sleeve. "I'm about done in. You care for a mug of beer?"

"Love to, but I need to see Ruben before he gets away."

"He won't get any farther than he already is—if you know what I mean." She shouldered her rake, and I started down the hill toward Navoe. "Garth Ryland?"

I turned. "Yes, Tillie?" I was hoping she'd tell me whom she'd seen.

"Nothing. I thought that was your name."

"I thought you had a question."

"Now that you mention it, maybe I do. Why the interest in Ruben?"

"Something I saw in a portrait. Something I read in a note. Something I saw in Fran Baldwin's face. Something that's gnawing at the back of my mind."

"What's that?"

"You ever put a jigsaw puzzle together?"

"Hundreds of them. That's about all I do come winter."

"Well, the first thing you have to do is turn over all the pieces. That's what I'm doing now, turning over pieces."

"Where does Ruben come in?"

"I'm not sure if anywhere yet. Is it true that he just snapped one night?"

"Like a pistol shot."

"Thanks, Tillie."

"Anytime . . . before sundown."

Ruben was bent over a tombstone, pulling the dead grass and weeds away from it. He had the single-minded concentration of an artist, and it was a pleasure to see the care he put into this simple task. Minutes passed before he acknowledged me. "Afternoon, Mr. Ryland."

"Afternoon, Ruben. I see they filled in Si's grave."

"Yes. They came today. They had to wait because of the snow."

"Get your birds fed?"

"Yes. The corn's all gone."

"The cemetery is shaping up. You've done a good job."

He glanced shyly at me, then continued working.

"What do they pay you, Ruben?"

"Nothing."

"Then why do it?"

"Somebody has to." He stood. It was the first time I'd seen him without his smile. Even his eyes had a spark of life. "You see, the dead . . . well, they don't have any place to go. I'm kind of the same way. So I spend most of my time here. I tend the stones and pull the weeds and mow the grass when it grows. This way the dead—they have a friend; and me—I have a home. It works out fine for both of us."

"Isn't it lonely out here?"

"What's lonelier, Mr. Ryland, alone by yourself, or alone with others? This way I don't have to know when they're laughing at me." He knelt and began pulling grass again.

"Who's laughing at you, Ruben?"

"Si Buckles. I heard him just the other night."

"What night was that?"

"The night they buried him, Mr. Ryland."

"Are you sure?"

"I'm sure." He said it in such a way that it left no doubt in my mind.

I watched him for a while, as the wind tousled his hair, and the sun cast an orange glare across his smooth, boyish face. Then the sun slipped behind a thick stand of woods, and Navoe was iced by a single shadow. I returned to Jessie and drove toward town. I got as far as Broken Claw where, below, the water was dark and smooth, whiskers of snow lingering along each bank. In the west pink sailboats of clouds floated in a pale-blue sky, while overhead the white hangnail moon had already crossed the meridian and started its descent. I shuddered. I was colder than I thought. I glanced back toward Navoe where night had already fallen, as an uneasy feeling began to grow in my guts. "Si Buckles lives." I took the note out of my pocket and dropped it into Hog Run. There! That was the end of that! But somehow I knew it wasn't.

I drove back to Oakalla, but didn't go home. This was Ruth's bowling night, and I didn't feel like being alone. Instead I went to the Corner Bar and Grill and drank my supper.

In the mirror I could see Sylvia Williams adjust her bra as she talked on the phone to her boyfriend. Meanwhile her three kids fought over a bag of potato chips. In the booth on my left a regular wearing a white T-shirt and a yellow tobacco smile and his tipsy female companion ate onion rings and washed them down with pitchers of beer. Someone was playing Willie Nelson on the juke box.

Herman Albright was on his tenth game of Electro-bowl. I was alone at the bar.

I stayed longer than I intended. I didn't drink that much, maybe four beers at the most. I just wasn't ready to go home to an empty house. Seven years since my divorce. I thought I'd be over it by now. And I was I guessed. No more stomach cramps, no more waves of nostalgia when I smelled someone's outdoor barbecue, no more fits of loneliness when I heard a woman laugh. But there was still something about an empty house I couldn't stand. I looked at the Hamm's clock above the bar. Midnight in the Land of Sky Blue Waters. Swirling the beer in my glass, I noticed it was warm.

Phil Chesterson burst in the side door of the bar. Completely drained of all color, he stood frozen a moment, like a terrified actor his first time under the lights, then sat beside me and ordered a double shot of bourbon. He drank it, as a hint of color returned to his face. He ordered another and drank this one more slowly.

"You okay, Phil?" I asked.

He jumped. He didn't even know I was there. "Yeah, I'm okay. It gets to me sometimes when I got a body on the slab and there ain't no one else there but me. I start seeing things."

"Who do you have on the slab?" I didn't remember anyone dying.

"You don't know him. He used to live here a long time ago. They shipped his body in yesterday." He held out his glass for another refill. "It's nothing new. It happens all the time. Even since Nam, I spook easy." His hand tightened on the shot glass. "Just give me a minute, and I'll be fine."

"You don't look fine."

"I'll be okay, I tell you!" He slapped the counter as if he'd suddenly remembered something. "Hey, I've got new pictures!" He fumbled for his wallet and finally got it where he could open it. He pointed to a photograph of him and his family posed around a Christmas tree. "Now,

Sarah, she favors her mother. And Tommy, he's like his old man, a real jock from the word go. And Sally, she's a tomboy, just like her Aunt Diana used to be. She can skin up a tree faster than any kid I ever saw."

I studied the photograph. I didn't remind him that I'd seen the same one on a Christmas card last December. I remembered because Sally, his daughter, had her Aunt Diana's impish smile. "So Diana was a tomboy," I said. "You'd never know it now."

He put his wallet away. "No, I guess you wouldn't." He slid his shot glass aside. "I have to be going, Garth. I should of been home by now." He left the way he came, as the bartender picked up his glass.

"Hiram, you ever seen him like that before?" I asked.

"Once. When his little boy got hit with that car."

"Not lately?"

"No. Not lately. When it comes right down to it, I never saw a man with a better set of nerves."

"That's what I thought. What do you suppose happened to him?"

"Hard to say. I get a lot in here that makes me ask that same question." He wiped the bar clean. "One thing I do know, he didn't go home."

"What makes you say that?"

He walked to the side door and looked out. "He left his truck here."

I got up and checked. "You're right. He did."

"Of course after three double shots I might forget where I was parked, too."

I walked back to the bar and sat down. "Hiram, if you didn't know Phil like you do . . . say he was some stranger who walked in off the street, what would you say he'd just seen?"

He never hesitated. "I'd say he'd just seen a ghost."

"Same here."

He wiped the bar in front of me. "Can I fill you up?" he asked. "Last one's on the house."

"Thanks, Hiram, but there's someplace I need to go."

I left the Corner Bar and Grill and started walking west. It was a still night, hardly a sound at all, and my footsteps seemed unnaturally loud as they padded against the sidewalk. I walked slowly, making sure I didn't step on any cracks. It was an old habit left over from childhood.

The houses in Oakalla's west end were beginning to show their age. A rotting pillar here, a shingle missing there, an ounce of neglect everywhere—until it became easier to buy and sell them cheap than to repair them. The houses themselves were sound, built to last in a time when nails and lumber were cheap, so neither was spared; and a two by four was a two by four, not a one and a half by a three and a half. And what they needed more than a coat of latex every few years was an owner who cared more about his house than his Grand Prix. But in Oakalla's west end the odds were against it.

I turned south off Jackson Street, cut through a vacant lot, and stopped short when I caught sight of the mortuary. A tower rising from one end, a turret guarding the other, and overgrown with bushes and ivy, it had the look of a Tudor castle gone to seed. There was nothing sinister about it. It was just a big old house that had outlived its prime. Imposing, though. Damned imposing.

I fought my way through the tangle of bushes and came out in a small clearing behind the mortuary. A light was on in the basement, so I knelt to look inside. The basement was empty. No Phil. No body. No ghost. But Phil said he'd been working on a body. That's what spooked him. If that were true, he had it hidden in the closet. I tried the door to the basement. Thankfully it was locked. I felt a shadow pass over me, as though a cloud had covered the moon. I glanced up. The sky was clear, the stars bright and bold, the moon nowhere to be found. I looked in every direction, but all I could see were bushes and trees and vines. I felt the hair rise on my neck and my skin go cold. It was time I went home. I'd stayed for one beer too many.

CHAPTER 4

The *Oakalla Reporter* came out early Friday morning. At noon I was still in my office answering the phone. I had enough requests to warrant a second edition, and I'd called my printer back in.

The door slammed, shaking the building, as Phil Chesterson strode into my office with a copy of the *Reporter* tightly rolled in his huge fist. Red from the roots of his hair to the tips of his fingers, he slammed the paper down on my desk. "Just what do you mean . . . *to be continued?*"

"What it normally means."

"That's a bunch of crap! I've got enough enemies in this town without you stirring them up every week!"

"Have you read the article?"

"No, but I've heard enough about it."

"Read it. I think you'll agree it could have been worse."

"And what about next week? Isn't that what *to be continued* means?"

"I have a story. I plan to run it until it's through."

"And when will that be—when they hang us from the highest rafter?"

"Hang you for what? I've been through most of those diaries. I haven't read anything yet that'll warrant a hanging."

He looked down, scuffing his shoe across the floor. "Just forget it, okay? Forget I even came in here."

"Fine with me. I've got a newspaper to run."

But he still didn't leave. "Did, wh . . . Did Si mention anything about . . . about what we had planned?"

"He mentioned something about it."

"What did he say?"

"Not much. None of the details if that's what you're worried about. What *did* you have planned anyway?"

He was trying his best to be casual. "We were going down to the pump house some night and put saltpeter in the city water. It never did come off."

"Why didn't it?"

He shrugged. "We just never got around to it."

"When was it supposed to come off?"

He thought a moment. "Friday. It was supposed to come off Friday. Si died before we had a chance to pull it."

"You drove Si to the hospital, didn't you?"

"Yeah, I drove him . . . me and Doc."

"Dead on arrival?"

"Ain't that what your paper said?"

"My paper didn't say. That's why I'm asking you."

"Well, that's what is was. Ask Doc." He was edging toward the door.

"You get home okay the other night?"

He stopped too quickly. "What night was that?"

"The night I saw you in the Corner Bar and Grill."

He seemed relieved. "Yeah, I got home fine. Like I told you then, I've been working too hard lately."

"You aren't in any real trouble, are you, Phil?"

"What makes you think that?"

"The diaries for one thing. Why are you afraid of them?"

"I ain't afraid of them!" His voice rose to a whine like a house dog locked out. "I've got a good business here, and a wife and family to think about. Do you think I want them to know the old man is an asshole? How would you feel if it was your life on those pages? You can't tell me you'd want it all spilled like a busted garbage bag."

"I'm not writing about you. I'm writing about Si."

"It amounts to the same thing. Hell, Garth, I know I ain't no saint, but I've never tried to hurt anyone or anything like Si did. So could you forget about next week? Give people time to simmer down a little?"

"I might . . . if you'll tell me what you saw the other night?"

Again he asked too quickly, "What night was that?"

"The same night we've been talking about, the night I saw you in the Corner Bar and Grill."

"I didn't see anything. I told you I've been working too hard lately." He was lying. It showed all over his face.

"And what about the body you had on the slab, the body that's never been buried yet?" I was giving him enough rope to hang himself.

"Oh, that's what's bothering you," he said genially. "A mistake. Even I had to laugh about it. They sent him to the wrong Oakalla. It should have been Michigan. His relatives were looking all over the country for him. I wondered why I hadn't heard from them and got to checking. They came for him yesterday."

"That explains it then."

He slapped my shoulder good-naturedly. "Sure. Everything's got a logical explanation." Then the wind rippled the window as his smile went sour, and he cast a hurried glance outside. *Everything*," he said, more to himself than to me.

An hour later I walked home. It was sunny and warm, shirt-sleeve weather, and the trees had a greenish cast, as if lightly brushed with pastels. There was a spring smell in the air, too, an earthy scent I'd never quite been able to define, but that brought back a lot of memories, a lot of smiles, and maybe a tear or two, as I counted all the springs that had gone before. Pure nostalgia. It was never that good—never as good as we remembered it. But today I really didn't give a damn. We dreamers never did.

I climbed the stairs to my study and picked up the diary

that Diana had found so fascinating. I'd been reading it off and on for two days, and all I'd found so far was eyestrain and a stiff neck. The pages were brittle and much of the writing smeared and nearly illegible. Also, Si Buckles wasn't the last of the late great poets, and his style had all the flair of a diet cola. Also, I was feeling a twinge of guilt, as if I'd been reading one of Diana's old love letters that I'd found while cleaning the attic. That was the thought that kept running through my mind. How do you ever bring the past to the present and understand either?

I was now reading a passage for the second time: "This willy . . ." No. "This will *be* the biggest one yet. The four of us will be waiting at Whyindot. Boy, he doesn't know what he's walking into! This is Fran's best plan, his baby. I wouldn't miss it for the world. Come on, tonight!" I glanced at the date: October 30, 1959. For some reason that should ring a bell.

"I thought I'd find you here." Ruth stood in the doorway of my study.

"I can't stay away."

"I don't see how a dead mole can be any more interesting than a live one."

"Did you read my column?"

"I read."

"What do you think now?"

"I don't think you should continue."

"Why?"

"It's a waste of your time."

"Maybe it is. But have you been outside?"

"Most of the day."

"What's it like?"

"Like it'll never rain again."

"There's one coming. I can smell it."

"The forecast is for fair and mild."

"I can't help it. It'll rain before morning."

"How sure are you?"

"I'll bet your next week's salary—you get double or nothing."

"You're on." She reached down and closed the diary I held. "Now, if you're through up here, you can help me carry in the groceries."

I opened the diary. "I'll be right down."

"Garth," she was staring at the diary, "what is it? What are you looking for? You're starting to give me the creeps."

"I won't know until I find it . . . if I find it."

"Do you have any idea?"

"No. But there's something rotten in Denmark, Ruth. I can feel it as sure as I can the rain that's coming. And I think you know I'm right."

She wheeled and started out of the room. "No comment."

I put the diary aside and followed her down the stairs. "What's going on around here? This isn't an inquisition."

She turned to face me. "The dead tell no tales."

"What's that supposed to mean?"

"Exactly what it says. There's nothing you can learn from Si Buckles."

"I think there is."

She sighed, giving me her sternest look. "Have it your way. But I'm warning you, Garth Ryland, some things are better left alone and these diaries are one of them."

"Why?"

"Call it premonition if you want. But with over fifty years on the farm I know a bad bull when I see one, and these diaries are a bad bull. You'd be smart to get rid of them now."

"Then I'm not very smart because I can't leave all these questions I have hanging on the wall. I'm going to answer them one way or another. I mean, who the hell was Si Buckles anyway? Just a small-town eightball? At least that's all he was a week ago. Now, I'm not so sure. The diaries seem . . . *seem*, mind you, the ramblings of a sick fool.

But I wonder. Don't you wonder, Ruth, at the purpose of them?"

She was backing away from me. I didn't realize I was stalking her. "I haven't read them," she said.

"You should. If you truly hated Si Buckles, you should. Because they lay him open like a skinning knife and spill his guts all over the pages."

The phone rang. I answered it, as Ruth retreated up the stairs.

"Garth?"

"Yes, Diana?"

"Can you come for supper?"

"Not tonight. I have some work to do."

"Scampi . . . bluepoints on the half shell. I drove all the way to Madison to get them." Her usual gaiety was gone. "I'll beg if you want me to."

"Diana, is something wrong?"

"I'll explain when you get here."

"What time?"

"As soon as you can make it."

"Give me time to shave and shower."

A few minutes later, as I walked across town, a red cirrus fan rose in the south and spread like rouge across the western sky. Grackles by the hundreds swarmed in to roost and settled like a black veil in the trees along Jackson Street. I noticed how quiet it was. No one but me was out and about. It seemed I was walking through a ghost town, and I couldn't say I liked the sensation.

We ate in the dining room on Diana's best china. Overhead, the chandelier threw rainbow sparkles as it giggled nervously in the breeze from the bay window. The only other sound was the scraping of our silver against our plates. I glanced at Diana, who glanced at Fran, who stared straight ahead, lost in a thought all his own. I wanted to speak, to break the silence that had followed me there, but it seemed the crystal would shatter if I did. Then Fran pushed away from the table and walked into his den, leaving his meal half eaten.

"What's wrong?" I finally asked Diana.

"I don't know. He's been like that all week. He's been missing appointments right and left until I finally had to leave word at his office not to take any more calls. He won't eat anything I fix, and I don't know when he sleeps. I thought maybe a little luxury would help." She looked at the food still on his plate. "Evidently it didn't."

"Do you want me to talk to him?"

"I don't know what I want. I don't know what he's after, my sympathy or what. I'm getting tired of it. That's all I know. I'm not in the mood to take care of him. I have my own problems at the moment."

"I'll see what I can do."

"You're more than welcome to try."

I entered his den. Fran was slumped in a leather chair facing the wall. His desk lamp was on, and it cast an eerie glow, making him seem even more distant than he was. Overhead on the wall was the muskie I'd helped him land. I recalled that September morning on the Flambeau, how his every fiber bristled with life as he fought the muskie in toward the boat, only to have it turn and make another run back toward the lily pads. Twice it jumped, completely clearing the water, and twice I thought he'd lost it. But when I finally swooped down with the net and dumped it at his feet, I knew it was ours forever. His fish. My memories of a man completely in love with life.

"That was a long time ago, Garth. A lifetime ago." He swung his chair around to look at me. "We should have stayed there on the Flambeau, you and I. Both our lives would be a lot happier. I wouldn't have to watch mine fall apart around me and you wouldn't be in love with my wife. She's not all peaches and cream, Garth. There beats an iron heart beneath that velvet breast. I'm giving you fair warning . . . as one friend to another."

"Fran, you're not making sense."

He smiled crazily and rolled his eyes until the whites showed. "Of course I'm not making sense." He began leafing through some papers on his desk. "Why don't you go back out and join the party?"

"Why don't you come with me?"

"No. Lately I've preferred my own company."

The door of the den swung open, and Phil Chesterson stood on the threshold like a walking dead man. He took no notice of me, but spoke to Fran as if he were the only one in the room. "I saw him again."

"Are you sure?" Fran asked.

"I'm sure."

"When?"

"A few minutes ago."

"Where were you?"

"Same place as last time."

"It couldn't be nerves?"

"Not three nights in a row."

"Can you go back there?"

"If you go with me."

"All right."

Phil was starting to lose control. "I'm sorry, Doc. I hate to come here like this. But I didn't know where else to go."

Fran put his hand on Phil's shoulder. "It's okay." I followed them into the kitchen where Diana was loading the dishwasher. "I have to be gone awhile," Fran said to her. "Why don't you make Garth a drink in the meantime?"

"I'll make us both one," she answered. "I think I'm going to need it." She closed the door of the dishwasher and set the controls. "Is it another emergency?" With just her voice she could cut deeper, faster than anyone I knew. "I've heard it said a leopard can't change his spots. Or in your case is it a laughing hyena?"

He slammed his fist into the wall. "Damn you! I told you I was done with that!"

She smiled in mockery. "Of course you are, Fran. You've said so, haven't you?"

He wanted to hit her. I could see his veins bulge and his knuckles turn white. Instead, he wheeled and left, as Phil followed him out the door.

I walked to the window and watched them drive away in Phil's truck. In the distance I could see lightning flicker like a snake's tongue and hear the grumble of thunder. "Do you know where they've gone?" I asked.

She sighed and threw up her hands. "I don't know. Unless it's the mortuary. It's sort of their lodge, where they go when they want to get away from everything."

"Do you want to come along?"

"I might as well. The evening's already shot."

We started walking west across town. In the distance the lightning continued to flash, one bolt after another streaking across the sky, while gradually the thunder deepened, shaking the ground like a giant's footsteps. Then the wind began to rise in the trees, and a ragged cloud tore loose from the main body of the storm and whisked by overhead, its shadow brushing the ground like a long black train. The moon disappeared. The air was suddenly cool.

The lights were on in the basement of the mortuary. Keeping to the shadows as we approached, we knelt in a soft patch of sod. Inside Fran and Phil were sitting at a card table and Phil was shuffling a deck of cards. Then Phil began to deal the cards.

"Satisfied?" Diana asked.

"Look closer."

"What do you mean?"

"At the table."

"I still don't see anything."

"There's a third chair. Phil is dealing it a hand."

"So?"

"The chair's empty!"

"Maybe they're expecting someone."

"Who?" A sudden gust of wind raked the leaves beside us.

"Garth, I feel stupid. Let's go back." I touched my finger to her lips for silence. "What is it?" she whispered.

"We're not alone." I'd seen a man's silhouette outlined by a flash of lightning. I pointed across the street. "Someone's standing behind that sycamore."

"Well, let him stand. I'm going home." She rose before I could stop her, and the silhouette disappeared.

"I'll be along in a minute," I said.

I crossed the street and looked behind the sycamore. No one there. I looked up and down the sidewalk. No one there either. The lightning flashed bolder, ripping a gold vein in the clouds. I timed the thunder. Four seconds. Less than a mile away.

Across the street Diana waited for me. I took her hand, and we began to run, as a swirl of leaves raced along the street beside us. Her hand suddenly tightened on mine. "Garth, I saw him, too!"

"Where?" I stopped to look.

She dragged me on. "Across the street. He's somewhere ahead of us."

We ran onto her front porch just as the rain cut loose, dropping a silver curtain across the street and hiding whoever was out there. We went inside and stood at the window. The rain came in waves, as the trees, bent by the wind, poked their bony shadows in our faces. Diana was deep in thought; then her eyes widened slightly and her hand covered mine. "*Si Buckles*," she whispered.

"What?"

"The man we just saw. He reminded me of Si Buckles."

"It couldn't be."

"I know." She was gazing intently out the window. "You saw him. Whom did he look like to you?"

"Someone familiar."

"Si Buckles?"

"I can't say. I only caught a glimpse." I followed her gaze. "See anyone out there?"

"No. Do you?"

"I suppose we both could be mistaken. That it's only our imagination."

She looked up at me, her eyes questioning. "But you don't think so, do you?"

"No."

"Why?"

"My eyes don't usually lie."

"Mine don't either. But it doesn't make sense. Why would anyone be following us?"

"He might not have been following us. He might have seen the light in the mortuary and then us running away. He might've wondered what was going on."

"That seems the logical explanation."

"Yeah. I wonder why I don't buy it." I glanced out the window. The rain had stopped as quickly as it began. "I've got to get back to my diaries. Will you be all right here?"

"Why wouldn't I be?"

"No reason, I guess."

I took a last look out the window, then walked to the phone and dialed. "Rupert, this is Garth."

"What is it?" he yawned.

"I'm at Diana Baldwin's. There's a prowler in the neighborhood."

"I'll be right over."

"Thanks, Rupert." I hung up. "I'll stay until he gets here."

"What was that for?" she asked.

"That's to ease my mind."

"Garth, I'll be fine."

"I won't be. I'll worry."

"Don't you think I can take care of myself?"

"I don't know. Can you? Say against a two-hundred-pound rapist?"

"He wasn't that big."

"A hundred-eighty-pound rapist then?"

"How big are you?"

"Somewhere close to that."

She smiled at me. "I could probably hold my own."

I nodded in agreement. "I'll bet you could."

When I saw Rupert's squad car outside, I left and started walking home. A block away I could see all the lights were on at home, even the one in the attic. I tried the back door. It was locked. I searched my pockets, but my keys were inside on my dresser. After knocking for five minutes, I began to yell. Ruth soon appeared at the door, brandishing my claw hammer. When she saw who it was, she lowered the hammer and let me in.

"Where have you been?" she asked, locking the door behind me.

"You wouldn't believe me if I told you." I began turning off lights. "What goes on here when I'm gone?"

"What are you doing?"

"Trying not to own R.E.M.C."

She was following me, turning the lights back on. "He might still be in here."

"*Who* might still be in here?"

"I didn't get his autograph."

"Do you want to start from the top?"

She sat down in her sewing chair, still holding the hammer. "Well, here it was ten-thirty, and you weren't home yet, so I fixed myself some popcorn and sat down to watch T.V. I wanted to watch Johnny, but he was gone, as usual, and when he's gone, it's like eating ham and beans without the ham, so I began to fidget and flip the dial, not paying much attention—when I heard something scratching around upstairs. At first I thought it was a mouse building a nest, but when the floor creaked, my hair stood straight out and my heart began to thump like a flat tire. I didn't know what to do. I tried to scream, but my throat was nailed shut, and I couldn't walk without tripping over myself, so I hit the volume on the T.V. Just at that time a lion growled and scared me and two thousand pygmies right out of our socks. Must've scared him, too, whoever it was, because I didn't hear another sound out of him. That's when I picked up the hammer and went looking."

"And you didn't find him?"

"Not a trace."

"Where could he have gone?"

"The window of your study opens right onto the porch roof."

"How would he know that?"

"You're the resident expert. Why do you ask me these questions?"

We went upstairs into my study. The window was closed, and there was no way to tell whether it'd been used or not. "You're sure someone was here?"

"Either that or we've got a two-hundred-pound mouse hiding in our attic."

"If that's the case, you'll need more than a hammer."

She suddenly looked down at the diaries on the floor. "No. It couldn't be."

"What couldn't be?"

She shook her head. "Nothing."

"Ruth . . . ?"

"Si Buckles' mother used to own this house. She and Si lived here until she bought her new one."

"Si Buckles is dead."

"That's what I keep telling myself."

I looked down at the diaries. "Ruth, have you been in these?"

"Are you serious? I get claustrophobia when I'm in the same room with them."

I picked up the diary for 1959. "I remember this one being on top. Don't you?"

"I don't know top from bottom and what's more I don't care." She handed me the hammer. "I'm going to bed."

"You say you heard him around eleven?"

"That's close enough. See you in the morning."

She left, as I took one more look around the room. Except for the diary, it was undisturbed, and I could have been wrong about the diary. I went downstairs and made a phone call.

"Hello?"

"Diana, this is Garth. What time was it when I left?"

"Around eleven-thirty. Maybe closer to twelve."

"Is Fran home yet?"

"Yes. He came in a few minutes ago. He's sleeping now."

"Did he say anything to you?"

"No more than he usually does. Why the questions?"

"Ruth said we had a night visitor. I'm trying to find out who."

"What kind of night visitor?"

"A prowler. Maybe the same one who followed us."

"Do you think it was Fran?"

"I don't see how it could have been. Sorry to bother you."

"No bother. You were on my mind anyway."

I hung up and went upstairs. Opeing the diary for 1959, I began to read. Two hours and one headache later I went to bed.

CHAPTER 5

The next morning I sat at the breakfast table staring at my overfried egg, while Ruth poured me half a cup of lukewarm coffee. Lifting the egg with my fork, I watched it bounce on my plate. "You have a steak knife?" I asked.

"Serves you right."

"I told you it was going to rain. You didn't have to bet with me."

"You were lucky, that's all."

"Do you want to forget the whole thing?"

"No. It'll be a lesson to me. You want another egg?"

"How much?"

"A dollar. Plus carrying charges."

"No, this one's fine."

"You realize it's going to cost you in the end?"

"I realize."

"Now, level with me. How *did* you know it was going to rain?"

"I smelled it."

"A likely story. What did it smell like?"

"Wet."

The phone rang. She answered it and handed the receiver to me. "Yes?" I asked.

"Garth, Rupert here. I'm out at Tillie's. Me and the cats and the dogs and the pig and the goat. Get away, now! Get away, you here! Hold on a minute, Garth. The goat's about to eat my hat!" I heard a scuffle; then he returned to the phone. "I'm going to have to make this short. I think old Billy's got his heart set on it. Tillie, call him off, will you! You still there, Garth?"

"Still here."

"I'd like for you to come out as soon as you can. Phil Chesterson just shot himself."

"At Tillie's?"

"No. Over in the cemetery."

"I'm on my way."

"I'll be looking for you."

"Who was that?" Ruth asked.

"Rupert."

"Is it as bad as you look?"

"I'll tell you later. Whatever you do, don't let those diaries out of your sight."

I drove to Navoe Cemetery. The first thing I saw was Ruben standing beside Phil's truck. He seemed lost, that he didn't know where to go or what to do. Rupert was waiting for me beside the wrought-iron gate that marked the entrance to the cemetery. He took my arm and led be aside. "You don't want to look. He used a shotgun." He glanced at Ruben who continued to stand by the truck, staring into the cab. "It won't hurt him none." We leaned against Rupert's car, as he pulled out a new tobacco pouch and showed it to me. "Birthday present . . . from Elvira." He picked his teeth with his thumbnail and spat on the ground. "You knew Phil pretty well, didn't you?"

"I knew him. I can't say I knew him well."

"As well as most?"

"I guess."

"Then you have any idea why he did this? He going broke? His wife about to leave him?"

"Not that I know of."

"What about his health?"

"He was fine as far as I know." Ruben was now walking

away from the truck. He still looked puzzled, as if death wasn't real to him. "Did you talk to Ruben?"

"Yeah. He heard the shot."

"When was that?"

"Hard to say exactly, since it's all the same time to Ruben. Sometime early this morning." Ruben had now disappeared into the woods. I was sorry. I wanted to talk to him. "Tillie heard the shot, too," Rupert said. "When it got light enough for her to see the truck, she called me."

"Where did the shotgun come from?"

"It's Phil's. He carried it in the truck."

"You want a gut feeling?" I asked.

"Go ahead."

"There's more to this than I want to know."

He pulled out a chew of tobacco and stared at it a moment before putting it into his mouth. "Yeah." A car pulled up beside Jessie. "Do you want to handle this one?" he asked.

Fran was already out of his car and walking toward the truck. I ran ahead to intercept him. "Fran, there's nothing you can do."

He continued walking. "Let me by, Garth."

"He's dead, Fran. He's beyond your help."

"I'm the doctor. I'll determine that." I caught his arm as he stiffened in resistance. "I said, let me by."

I stepped aside, as he walked to the truck. Throwing open the door, he pitched forward, then caught himself. Braced with one arm against the cab, he swung the other like a club, breaking out the side window. "Fran?" I called. He didn't answer.

"Fran, let's take a walk."

He let me lead him, and we circled the cemetery twice before he shook loose, and I let him go on his own. He walked to Si Buckles' grave. Kneeling amidst the dried flowers and wreaths, he dug his hands into the soft earth and let it spill a few grains at a time through his fingers. He was there a long time, long enough for the sun to clear the woods and send its first runners of light across Navoe. Then he rose and walked back to his car. I joined him there.

"Will you tell Diana for me?" he asked.

"I think you should."

"I can't. If she goes to pieces, I'll go to pieces. She's always been the stronger."

"All right. But don't you think it's time you tell someone what's going on?"

"Why? So he can end up like Phil? Leave it alone, Garth. I tried to tell you before. Leave it alone!"

"I won't leave it alone. Phil's dead and I feel I'm partly responsible, and it's going to be a long time before I can sleep nights. Longer, if I don't get to the bottom of this."

"You're not responsible," he said quietly. "It would have happened anyway, with or without your newspaper. It didn't begin with you, and it won't end with you, and there's not a damn thing you can do to stop it, so from now on just stay out of it."

"What about Diana, is she involved?"

"No, she's not involved." But he wasn't very convincing. "Look, Garth, I know the score between you two, and I know that if something happens to me, you'll be the first one she'll turn to. But even though it hurts like hell to ask, I'm asking one favor. Never let me know, will you? Never let me know you've slept with her. There are some things a man can't know and stay sane." He smiled to himself, as he gazed at the powder-blue sky. "Have a nice day." He climbed into his car and drove away.

Rupert soon joined me. He held up a piece of broken glass, using it like a mirror to bounce the sun's rays off Tillie's roof. "You know, Garth, it doesn't figure. A man of forty—a young man really—a good business, a nice wife and kids. And here it is spring, the peepers chanting from every sinkhole, the new-grass scent so bold you can reach out and touch it . . . and he cashes in his chips. I might see it come late fall or winter, a north wind staring you in the face. But now? Now it's almost *criminal*." He dropped the glass at his feet. "What was he into, Garth? You got any idea at all?"

"Some. I'm chipping away at it."

"Chip faster. I don't like the vibrations from here." He watched the ambulance from Operation Lifeline wind its way down the road toward us. "It's a miracle. They made it before noon. I'm surprised they don't have their siren on." He sighed. "I'd better get out to the road and flag them down. Anything you need to tell me?"

"Not now."

He tipped his hat. "Until you do." He began to run. "Now, where are those fools going?"

A few minutes later I stood at Tillie's door. One hound had ahold of my pants leg, gently tugging on it while another was lying across my feet. The other two were lined up behind the first, waiting their turn at me. I guessed I should have felt honored. Tillie stepped outside, routing them as she did. "You should have given them a good swift kick," she said.

"I never kick a dog," I said. "He might remember next time."

"Not if you kick hard enough. What can I do for you?"

"Sheriff Roberts said you're the one who called him."

"First thing this morning."

"Any particular reason?"

"Ain't a corpse reason enough?"

"You saw him then?"

"Nope. I heard the shot and saw the truck. That was enough for me."

"Was Ruben there then?"

"He was just coming up to the truck. He took a look inside and sort of backed away like he'd got ahold of a hot wire. That's when I made the phone call."

"Ever see the truck before?"

"I thought we were coming to that. It looked like the same truck that belonged to the graverobbers. Don't quote me, though. Things look different in the moonlight. People, too."

"You hear anything else besides the shot? A door slamming or someone talking?"

"The dogs barked. That's what woke me up."

"Nothing else?"

"Nothing else."

"Thanks, Tillie."

"Shame, ain't it, a young man like that? When I was his age, I felt like I'd barely turned the tap."

"How old are you, Tillie?" I'd always wanted to know.

"Seventy-three. Give or take a year. Had a record of it, but Billy ate the family Bible, and that's where it was. I don't have as much trouble remembering the year I was born as the year I'm in. About the time I get used to one, another comes along. After a while they run together."

"Same here."

"Children. I think that's what I miss more than anything. You can kind of mark time by them—when they took their first step, their first day of school, their first real date. I had three. One's dead. The other two are in California. They say they want me to move out there, but that's to ease their conscience about leaving home. We both know they've got enough kooks in California now. One more might sink it."

"Ever been there?"

"Nope, and I don't plan on it."

"I like it."

"Then what are you doing in Oakalla?"

"I like it better here."

She gazed around her farm. "I wouldn't drive off the road to see it, but it's home. It's easy to find fault with, but hard to leave, if you know what I mean." The pig stuck its head out the screen and gave a loud snort. "Ambrose, mind your manners!" She bopped him on the nose, as he ducked inside. "Do you want some advice from crazy old Tillie, the zoo keeper?"

"As long as I don't have to take it."

"Say that was the same truck I saw the other night and say Phil Chesterson is as dead as I think he is. Navoe might be a good place to stay away from for a while."

"Do you know something I don't?"

"I know a lot of things you don't . . . but then I've lived longer."

I could almost see her mind working. She would tell me only what she thought I should know. "Tillie, you'd make a good reporter. You know how to protect your sources."

"It's not a matter of protection. It's a matter of survival. You learn the knack after seventy years . . . or you don't make it that far."

"Do you mind if we back up a few steps?"

"You've got a one-track mind, you know that. My Albert was the same way. The house could have fallen down around him, nearly did on one occasion, and he'd have gone right on making love. So what's your question?"

"Well, say that was Phil Chesterson's truck the other night and say Phil Chesterson was driving it, isn't it entirely possible that Fran Baldwin came along for the ride?"

"It's entirely possible. But again don't quote me."

"I wouldn't think of it. Thanks, Tillie." I left her standing on the porch and drove back to town.

I told Diana about Phil. I didn't want to. I'd never been a good bearer of bad news. Maybe I should've put on an elf suit and done a little soft shoe before delivering the blow. Maybe then it would seem less real. I didn't know. When I died, I hoped they send all those concerned an engraved invitation to the cremation. Old English letters engraved in gold. "Brave Garth just bit the dust. We'll roast the sonofabitch at ten."

When I told her, Diana walked to her bay window and stared outside. Then she took one deep, sudden breath and held it until I thought she'd explode.

"Diana?"

She let it go. "I'm okay."

"You're sure?"

"I'm sure." She turned to face me, blinking back the tears. "What's there for me to say? That I'm sorry? I'm sorry, Phil. Can you hear me? I don't think he can."

"Do you want me to stay?"

"No, I'll be all right."

"It's not over, Diana. Fran told me as much himself."

"What's not over? Don't talk in riddles to me, Garth."

"I don't know. All I do know is that it has its roots somewhere in the past. But do me a favor, will you? See if you can find Fran. I think you need each other right now."

"I'll make some phone calls. Where will you be?"

"At home."

"More diaries?"

"I'm afraid so."

"I wish you wouldn't."

"I don't think I have a choice now."

I drove home and climbed the stairs to my study. The diaries waited for me inside. I didn't open them right away. I couldn't. Every time I tried I thought of Phil Chesterson. A shotgun. The only thing worse was a guillotine.

Hours later, after wading through hundreds of pages of Si Buckles' scrawl, I stopped to focus my eyes, to make sure I still *could* focus my eyes. I leaned back against the metal chest. I was getting nowhere. All I'd read so far was beside the point. It seemed only one of his diaries applied—his last. The last laugh. Just what the hell was it anyway?

Ruth came in carrying a ham sandwich and a glass of milk. "How's it coming?" she asked.

"Slow." I reached for my wallet, remembering she was out a week's pay because of our bet. "What do I owe you?"

"It's on the house tonight."

"Thank you." I closed my eyes. "I'm going to be seeing Si Buckles in my sleep." She didn't answer. I looked up to see her staring at her hands. "Ruth?"

"It wouldn't help him anyway," she said to herself.

"*What* wouldn't help him?"

She flustered. "Nothing. I was thinking out loud." She picked up the tray and left.

I began reading Si Buckles' last diary, the entry two weeks before his death: "I wonder what it feels like to die, if it all goes black and cold, or if there really is a soul that's cut loose to find its way to a better life. I wonder if anyone will miss me. I have this dream sometimes where I have my funeral and nobody comes. Here I am, all dressed up with no place to go. Come to think of it, that's kind of been my life. It seems I've been waiting in the wings forever. So maybe death's not so bad after all . . . and maybe heaven is the end of loneliness." I set the diary down. Something was wrong here. Not a comma out of place, not a word misspelled, and clearly, not the words of a fool.

The phone rang. Ruth called up the stairs. "For you."

"Who is it?"

"Diana."

"I'll be right down." I cleared a path through the diaries and went downstairs. "Did you find him?"

"No. I've called everywhere. Either someone's lying or he doesn't want to be found."

"Have you tried Maryanne?"

"Yes. She and the kids are here now."

"Have you talked to her about Phil?"

"Yes. She doesn't know anything either, only that he was deeply disturbed about something."

"Does she remember when it started?"

"Wait a minute. I'll ask her." Ruth was watching intently from the kitchen. She had more than a passing interest in this. "The night of the snowstorm," Diana said. "He wasn't the same after that."

"Thanks, Diana. I'll go looking for Fran now."

"I'd go with you, but I hate to leave Maryanne alone."

"It's okay. If I find him, I'll send him home." I hung up.

"Well," Ruth asked, "what was that all about?"

"Fran Baldwin is missing."

She threw up her hands. "That's it! Those diaries get a new home first thing tomorrow!"

"Over my dead body."

"Have it any way you like."

"They're staying here, and you're making sure of it."

"I'd rather sit with a time bomb."

"You'll be fine."

"And where will you be?"

"Looking for Fran."

"If I were you, I'd leave him lost."

"What is it you don't like about him anyway?"

"I never liked his looks. He's too pretty to suit me."

"That's all, his looks?"

"From where I stand, that's enough. Coming up the hard way, Garth, I've never trusted anyone who was born with a silver spoon in his mouth."

It was warm outside, warm enough for me to hear the creak of a porch swing and see moths darting about the street lights. I went to the Corner Bar and Grill first. No one there had seen Fran. I made the rounds of his friends, and he wasn't with any of them either. That left one place for me to go. The mortuary.

I took a shortcut down a back alley bordered on both sides by a sprawling hedge. It made me uneasy. I didn't like tunnels—green or otherwise. Not since I had one collapse on me in the heart of Grandma Ryland's haymow. I came out in the backyard of the mortuary just as a light came on in the basement. I looked away and back again. The light was still on.

Crossing the yard, a queen-size spider web clinging to my face, I climbed down the cellar steps to the basement. It was then I saw Fran lying on the mortuary slab. My heart missed a beat, my foot forgot to track, and I lost my balance, crashing into the door. Fran rose at the sound and stared straight at me. I opened the door and went inside.

"Frightening, isn't it, a visitation from the dead?" he asked calmly. "It wouldn't take many to unnerve you."

"What the hell are you doing?"

"Waiting."

"For whom?"

"Just waiting."

"Fran, you're not making sense."

"I'm making perfect sense. You're just not understanding very well. Perhaps you need to spend more time with your diaries."

"Look, I know you're under a strain . . ."

"You have no idea what I'm under, my friend." He lighted a cigarette, watching the smoke rise to the ceiling in a cirrus haze. "I hated Si Buckles, did I ever tell you that? I hated him like I've hated no other man." He laughed. "And the poor fool never even knew it."

"Then why did you put up with him?"

"Convenience. Simple convenience. If you searched the entire earth, where could you find a more perfect dupe? Most men have to learn what for Si came naturally."

"I've read those diaries, Fran. Over and over again. Who was really the dupe? Who's sitting on a mortuary slab while his wife is waiting at home for him?"

He smiled. "Ah, yes, sweet Diana, the faithful one. Would you tell her I won't be home tonight?"

"You tell her yourself."

"I'm sorry, but I can't leave. I have an appointment here."

"I'll keep it for you."

"You don't even know who's coming."

"I really don't give a damn. I'd rather sit here myself than try to explain to Diana why you aren't coming home."

"Why explain anything? Why not let me hang myself?" He challenged me, "Who's the fool now?"

I shrugged. "I gave you your chance. If you want to throw open your bedroom door, I'm not afraid to walk in."

He said quietly, "I'll kill you if you do."

"Then go home to her. If you can still feel that, you have no business here."

"Why the concern? You don't owe me anything. In truth it's the other way around. You've been a better friend to me lately than I to you. Are you trying to ease your conscience to make up for loving Diana?"

"I'm trying to save your life. Diana has nothing to do with it."

He studied me carefully. "Just how much do you know?"

"I know you went with Phil Chesterson to Navoe Cemetery last Sunday night."

"And . . . ?"

"And whatever it was you saw there brought all of this on."

"And what was that?" He was so calm it was unnerving.

"I don't know. I was hoping you'd tell me."

"I gave you good advice, Garth, my professional best. Leave it alone." He walked past me to the door. "But since you insist, you *will* stay until midnight? I'll expect a report tomorrow."

"Yes, I'll stay."

"I'm not crazy, Garth, some sicko you have to humor. The only reason I'm letting you stay is because I know he won't come with you here."

"*He?*" But he didn't answer.

I stayed until after midnight, watching the moths dust the windows and the sweat seep from the basement walls. Fran was right. No one came. I didn't know why, but I half expected him to. As I closed the door and started up the concrete steps, I turned for one long look at the mortuary, stern and imposing like the dark hull of a freighter. I couldn't believe I'd just spent an evening there. With that kind of courage I could have made Eagle Scout.

Phil Chesterson was buried in Navoe. A note had been found in his truck requesting it. I looked at Phil's family gathered around him for the last time and wished there was someplace else for me to be. I wasn't a good mourner. I hadn't cried, really cried, since I was fifteen when my dog died, and I sometimes doubted if I'd ever cry again. I should have hired my Aunt Bessie as a stand-in. She'd cried at every wedding, funeral, and christening she'd ever been to, and one mortuary in her hometown had even issued her a standing invitation. It looked so easy when she cut loose. I wondered why I'd never learned the knack. Maybe because I was afraid that once I started, I'd never be able to stop.

Fran was a pallbearer and stood up well under his burden. He was a handsome devil, even in mourning. Tall and straight and proud, he was what I once wished I'd look like . . . before I realized the game was five-card stud, not five-card draw.

Diana stood beside me with her hand lightly resting on my arm. I didn't know what her thoughts were. I knew her eyes were dry and head was up and that she could be one tough lady when she wanted to be. When the service ended, we walked across the cemetery to the edge of the woods beyond. It was another warm day, and the scent of wildflowers came from the woods, while overhead a mourning cloak hovered momentarily, then darted into the sun and was gone. The only sound was that of a raincrow drumming the same mournful note over and over again.

Diana leaned against a tree with her head back and the sun streaming into her face. "Come closer," she said. I did. "Closer. I want to feel you here." I did as she asked, and though we never touched, we were as close at that moment as two people could be. "Will you drive me home?"

"What about Fran?"

"He's riding back with Maryanne."

I looked back across the cemetery. Everyone had left, except for Ruben, who stood alone beside Phil's grave. "In a minute." I touched my hand to hers. "I'd like to talk to Ruben?"

"Go ahead."

I left her there and walked to where Ruben was standing with his scythe. He was engrossed in a thought, his face solemn like a warrior fasting. "Afternoon, Ruben."

He looked up and smiled. "Afternoon, Mr. Ryland."

"A penny for your thoughts."

His smile faded. "You know, you're the first person to ever say that to me, the first person who ever thought I had any worth hearing." He righted a small, plastic flag that had been knocked over. "You wanted to ask me something, Mr. Ryland?"

"A couple things, Ruben. Have you seen Si Buckles lately?"

He saw an urn that had been toppled and moved to right it. "Si Buckles is dead, Mr. Ryland."

"I know. I just thought you might have seen him."

"That would be hard, wouldn't it, Mr. Ryland?"

"I'm sorry. I shouldn't have asked."

He brightened. "I don't mind. I don't get the chance to answer many questions." He was looking straight at me, but seemed to see only the woods beyond. Then I remembered Diana was behind me. "You said you had a couple things to ask me?"

"You're the one who found Phil, aren't you?"

"Yes, I'm the one."

"Did you see or hear anything before the shot?"

"I heard the truck drive up."

"How long before?"

"I'm not good with time, Mr. Ryland." He indicated west. "Long enough for the moon to go from there to there." He pointed to show me.

"Did you hear a door slam?"

"No. That's why I didn't come sooner."

"Then Phil was alone?"

"I didn't see anyone else." He was still looking through me. "Mr. Ryland?"

"Yes, Ruben?"

"That's Diana Chesterson over there."

"Yes. Only she's Diana Baldwin now."

"That's right. She's Fran's wife." He continued to stare at her. "She was always a real lady, Mr. Ryland. You know, the kind men die for." He looked away, his gaze distant. "I'd have died for her once. I really would have."

"No longer, Ruben?"

"What?" I'd pulled him back from somewhere in the past.

"You'd no longer die for her?"

His smile was turned inward, like the smile Diana painted on him in his portrait. "Oh, she belongs to someone else now. But I still come by her house every now and then to see her. I hope you don't mind."

"Why should I mind?"

"I see you there sometimes. I see you here with her today. You seem to fit together, like the wings of a butterfly. You know that, Mr. Ryland? He can fly for thousands of miles and sit on the leaf of a clover. There's nowhere a butterfly can't go with both his wings."

— 79 —

I clasped his shoulder. It was hard, like knotted hemp. "I have to go."

Diana waited for me, handing me a bouquet of dandelions. "My favorites," I said, as we began to walk.

"I thought so."

"I mean it. I like dandelions. They're the soldiers of spring."

"So do I. That's why I picked them."

"What are you holding behind your back?"

"Bend over and close your eyes."

"Why?"

"Just do as I say."

I did, as she hung a dandelion chain around my neck. "You've been busy."

"I had to do something. What were you and Ruben talking about for so long?"

"Clovers, butterflies . . . other beautiful things."

"He's a fascinating guy when you take the time to listen to him."

We got in her Bentley and began to drive. "Yes, he is."

"I was thinking. I see Ruben and I see Fran and I see you, and in doing so, I see myself. Ruben is my conscience, Fran is my spirit, and you are my soul. I wonder how I could paint that?"

I stopped in front of Tillie's. "I'll be back in a minute."

"Your chain."

"What?"

"Take your dandelion chain off."

"I doubt if Tillie will mind."

Tillie stepped outside and waited for me on the porch. She wore her bonnet, apron, and ankle-length dress even though I was sweating in shirt sleeves. The hounds and Billy lay in a semicircle in the shade at the foot of the porch, and a Siamese cat was perched on the eave ready to pounce on one of them. I side-stepped the hounds and jumped onto the porch before all hell broke loose—which it did a moment later as cat, dogs, and goat made one orbit of the yard and disappeared into the woods. "I'm back," I said to Tillie when the dust cleared.

"I see you are." She looked down the hill where Diana waited. "Who's your friend?"

"Diana Baldwin."

"Her car or yours?"

"Hers."

"It's a Bentley, isn't it? Thirty-seven, thirty-eight?"

"Thirty-six."

"Never owned one. Always wanted to, though." She clicked her tongue in regret. "Sorry now I didn't." Then she turned to me. "What's on your mind?"

"Promise you won't laugh."

"Scout's honor."

"I'm looking for Si Buckles. Have you seen him lately?"

"What kind of question's that, to find out for sure if I'm nuts?"

"No, it's to see if I am."

"You're serious, aren't you?"

"Deadly."

She led me across the porch. "Here, you'd better sit in the shade awhile."

"I take it then you haven't seen him?"

"Nope, I haven't seen him. But if I do, he'd better have his chubby legs in gear or they'll have to bury him again. Lord knows once of him was enough." She squinted at me. "You think he's escaped the grave?"

"That's what I've been told."

"Then you better check your sources. It's that kind of talk that keeps me up at night. Who told you anyway?"

"Phil Chesterson."

"Any relation to the one they just buried?"

"The same."

"And one more good reason to stay away from Navoe."

"You're here, aren't you?"

"That's different. I'm part of the woodwork. Ain't nobody going to mind crazy old Tillie. Me and Ruben, we

— 81 —

staked our claims long ago." She smiled, "But you—you're smarter than the average bear. Ghost or flesh, if I was up to something, I wouldn't want you nosing around."

"I'll try to keep a low profile."

She looked down at the yellow Bentley. "I see you are. And, of course, that's your mother in the front seat." She shook her head and went to rescue the cat now treed by the hounds at the edge of the woods.

I walked back down the hill. Diana had her head resting on the seat and her eyes closed. She looked younger than thirty-seven, more like seventeen with her dandelion bracelet on one hand and my bouquet in the other. Her eyes opened and she smiled. "I'm glad you weren't going to be gone long."

"I'm sorry. I had something I needed to ask her."

"I don't mind. The way I feel now, I don't care if I ever go back. I feel clean today, Garth, cleaner than I have for a long time. There's no pretense with you, nothing I have to hide." She opened the door for me. "So take the long way home."

We rode with the top down, as the dust rolled with the car and the sun burned our faces. We drove past small woodlots, white with budding dogwoods, through a rumbling covered bridge, and along Hog Run, which raced in chocolate swirls beside us. It seemed like old times—very old times, long before I knew Diana—when I had a '55 Chevy convertible and the world by the tail. We came to a wide spot in the road that had once been some kind of settlement and was now overgrown with weeds and brambles. I slid the Bentley to a stop. "It was here! I'm sure of it!"

Diana sat up in the seat. "*What* was here?"

"The haunted house! The one that used to scare the hell out of me! Don't you remember it?"

I remembered because I had to ride my bicycle by here at night on my way home from town. About a quarter-mile away I'd start pedaling like hell, so by the time I reached here I was going flat out with the spokes humming and the tires smoking. Then with a wary eye cast over my shoulder to see who might be following, I slid to a running stop in Grandma Ryland's yard and sprinted for the front door, all the time praying it wasn't locked.

She leaned back and closed her eyes. "Vaguely. I believe it burned."

I sat staring at the underbrush that had reclaimed the settlement. "Willow? Winona? It began with a W. What was it's name?"

"Wyandotte."

"Wyandotte! That's it! Now where have I heard that name lately?"

She pointed to a green road sign. "Read it."

I did. We were on Wyandotte Road. "But I never read road signs."

She lightly tapped the dash with her fist. "Drive on, James."

I drove on. "Yes, my lady." Though I still wondered where I'd heard the name Wyandotte.

Grandma's farm had changed from the farm I remembered. The Leghorns and the Guernseys and the Hampshires were gone. So were the woodshed and most of the trees in the apple orchard. Her pride and joy, an immaculate flower and vegetable garden that in some years seemed like it could have fed the world, had gone to seed with only a few volunteers straggling up each year to remind me of my neglect.

I now rented the ground to a neighbor, who plowed everything that wasn't moving and occasionally some of the things that were. He wanted to tear out all the fence rows, bulldoze the woods, and make the farm into a giant corn field. I wouldn't let him. I liked to hear the quail call in the evening and measure a buck by the height of his scrape. I liked to see raccoon tracks in the mud along the creek and kick a cottontail out of hiding just to watch him run. These things had no price. They couldn't be bought with a few bushels of corn.

We left the Bentley under a white oak, climbed the gate, and walked through the pasture to the pond, spring fed and nestled in cottonwoods. In the distance we could see the flash of the renter's tractor, and the air was fragrant with the scent of freshly turned earth. We stood a moment overlooking the pond, our shadows rippling in the dark-green water. Then Diana unzipped her dress. "It's been years since I've been skinny-dipping," she said. Her dress fell to her ankles. "How about you?" She stepped out of her dress and kicked off her shoes. Next came her bra and pants, which she dropped at my feet. "Well, are you coming or not?" she challenged me.

"Coming," I said, unbuttoning my shirt. Though I knew better.

The first surge of cold water took my breath away. I spent the next few minutes gasping for it. After that I was too numb to care. We took turns splashing each other, played a game of water tag, and staggered for the shallows when we were too tired to go on.

Diana rested on her hands and knees, her eyes closed, her head hanging down until her hair just touched the water. She had a magnificent body. Supple and slender and sleek as an otter, she radiated life. I stared at her a long time before slipping back into deep water and diving for the bottom. It was better I didn't think about it.

When we got out, we dried in the sun, as it went from yellow to scarlet to purple. Diana lay with her head in my lap. I chewed on a clover, watching the swallows dimple the surface of the pond while they dived for mosquitoes. Then together we watched the sun set. It didn't matter the air was now cool on our naked bodies, or that the renter was now chugging up the lane toward us. It was as though we were the first, and last, man and woman on earth, and time for the moment waited on us.

She sighed—a sigh I knew too well. "It's so peaceful

here. It's hard to believe there's a world out there
. . . that I buried my brother this morning. I'm the last
now, the last of what was once a family. For some reason
that makes me feel old."

"Tillie says it's her children she misses most."

She smiled wistfully, walking her fingers down my leg.
"That might be what I'm missing, too. I've never had any. I
don't feel guilty, that I've somehow failed as a woman. But
I'll see one sometimes—you know, a toddler all dressed up
in her pink bonnet, and I'll just want to mother her to
death." Her smile was distant. "I almost had one—long
enough to feel her move inside me. It was a good feeling,
Garth. After I lost her, it didn't go away for a long time."

"Why didn't you try again?"

"By then I wasn't sure I wanted to. Not that Fran and I
couldn't make beautiful babies, but that's not really fair, is
it? To make a baby to save a marriage that you can't?" She
looked up at me. Her eyes were sheathed in a strange
light. "Funny, Garth, but I think I'd like to have your baby.
Someday."

I looked away toward the white farmhouse that held so
many happy memories for me. When Grandma died, it
seemed the heart went out of it. But lately I'd thought
about moving back here. Not alone, though. And probably
not very soon. Someday. Life was always going to come
together . . . someday.

I felt her shudder. "You cold?" I asked.

"A little."

"I'll get your things."

"There's no hurry."

The peepers had begun to sing from the pond. In the
east the moon rose white and round, while strands of
cirrus, as fine as angel hair, were weaving a web in the
west. She was right. There was no hurry. Days like this
came once a millennium.

Finally we drove back to town, stopping in her driveway.
"You sure I can't take you home?" she asked.

"No, I'd rather walk. It'll help me come down easy."
She gave me a sisterly kiss. "Well, thanks for today."
"You, too."

I walked home. The web of cirrus had begun to spread, and the moon now hung in an orange net of clouds. Ruth had supper ready and was pacing the kitchen, clutching a gravy ladle in her right hand. She reminded me of a sergeant confronting a squad of new recruits. "Where have you been?" she asked before I'd even closed the door.

"The funeral."

"For six hours? It doesn't take that long to bury the pope."

"We took a drive afterwards."

She began mashing the potatoes with a vengeance. "Pour some milk in here, will you?"

"Sure. Say when."

"When!" She jerked the pan out from under me, as the milk spilled on the stove. "I didn't say drown them." The stench of scalded milk began to fill the kitchen. Holding the potatoes in one hand, she opened a window with the other. "And I take back everything I said about Si Buckles. He wasn't a mole. He was a demented weasel."

"Have you been reading his diaries?"

"What if I have?"

"I thought you said you'd rather read a Kleenex box."

"I changed my mind."

"Did you find anything I should know?"

"Nope. I don't even know what I read. I kept telling myself one more page and I'd quit. One page became ten and ten became twenty and after that I lost count. It gets to you after a while—like trying to sew a featherstich." She set the mashed potatoes on the table. "I know one thing, though. I'd give my eyeteeth to learn what the last laugh was."

"Phil said they were planning to put saltpeter in the city water supply," I said, as we sat across from each other at the table.

"Then he lied because they already did that."

"You're sure?"

"Sure I'm sure. About ten years ago. Had most of the men around here checking out their plumbing."

"I wonder why Phil would lie?"

"Force of habit maybe. How's the chicken?"

"Fine."

"The gravy?"

"It'd be better without the giblets."

"I'll remember next time."

"You knew him better than I did. Was Phil in the habit of lying?"

"No. He wasn't any good at it. It takes some imagination to be a good liar."

"Which brings me to my next question. What do you have planned this evening?"

She looked at me suspiciously. "Nothing. Why?"

"I've read every one of those diaries. I didn't read about the saltpeter. I want you to see if you can find it."

"What's the matter, don't you believe me?"

"Sure, I believe you. Why shouldn't I?"

"Then why the double-check?"

"I always double-check my sources."

"And if I don't find it?"

"I'll still believe you."

She gave me the fisheye. "Okay, what's your angle?"

"No angle. I just need your help."

"Why didn't you just ask for it in the first place?"

I gave her a knowing smile. "Because I knew better."

After supper I changed clothes and put on my blue windbreaker, which had gone out of style and come back in again in the years that I'd owned it. Like everything else I owned, it'd seen better days, and I couldn't have given it to the Salvation Army, but it was comfortable—damned comfortable—and dark. And tonight especially I wanted it to be dark.

I glanced out the window. Just my luck. It'd started to rain. "I won't be gone long," I said to Ruth.

"I've heard that one before. I'll leave a light on."

I walked uptown. All the buildings were dark, except for the Corner Bar and Grill, which leaked a smoky, yellow light. I looked inside. Fran wasn't there. I didn't expect him to be. I walked on and soon was in sight of the mortuary. Ahead, its tower grey and solemn, its face blurred by the rain, the mortuary reminded me of a gothic Rorschach. I didn't believe in ghosts. Except for God according to Garth, I didn't believe in the supernatural, but I couldn't look at the mortuary without feeling uneasy. Conditioning. That's all it was. The bogeyman, the Mummy, and the Shadow had all left their mark on me. There was no reason to be afraid. I knew that. But it was hard to intellectualize raw, primitive fear, especially when it was staring me right in the face. My first instinct was to run, ask questions later. Except I was too old to run, and that was the crux of my problem.

Fran sat alone at the card table playing solitaire. His movements were slow, heavy, and when he glanced my way, he looked like an old man, a fisherman perhaps whose fingers pondered over the knots that he once tied so nimbly in his youth. My heart went out to him. A few hours earlier at Phil's burial he looked like the patron saint of Oakalla. I found the dryest spot around and settled in.

Hours later the rain finally stopped, though the water continued to drip softly around me. Fran still sat at the card table, and I sat hunched in a shadow. Rising, I stretched out the kinks and checked my watch. Two A.M. I must be crazy. A dog began barking in the next block east, and another soon joined it. The barking grew closer, more frenzied, then nothing. I waited. The moon shimmered once and went back under a cloud. I stared ahead, wishing I could peel back the night. Fran had heard the dogs, too, and now stood at the basement door with his face pressed to the glass. He appeared a caricature, a parody of the man I once knew.

Several minutes passed. My eyes began to water as the damp air settled into me. I had to move. When I did, the spell was broken, and one of the dogs started barking again. This time, though, the barking grew progressively fainter and finally died altogether.

At four A.M. Fran left. I was too tired to follow. I found a dry spot under a maple, leaned against its trunk, and closed my eyes. When I opened them again, a bird was chirping overhead, and a sliver of red showed through the grey in the east. Rising unsteadily, every muscle in my body with its own separate ache, I started home. I'd gone a block east, about to where I first heard the dogs, when I saw a lump in the street ahead of me. Approaching it, I discovered a dog, a trickle of blood dried on its lip, a half smile, half snarl on its face. Apparently hit by a car, it'd died without a yelp. I dragged it off the street into the grass and hoped it wasn't some kid's pet. Funny, I didn't remember seeing a car on that street all night.

At home Ruth sat in her favorite chair asleep before the television. I shut off the set and pulled up a chair facing her. Then I tickled her nose. She swatted at me and missed. I tickled it again. She swatted and missed again. The third time I left my hand there, catching hers when she swung. Her eyes and mouth flew open at the same time. I had to laugh. "Garth Ryland, you do that again, and you'll be a candidate for the Purple Heart!" She shook all over. "Brrr. I thought he had me for sure."

"*Who* had you?"

"Si Buckles, who else?"

"Why Si Buckles?"

She flustered. "Why? Because I just spent half the night reading his drivel. That's why. Can you think of a better reason?"

"I was just asking." I picked up the diary lying beside her. "Did you find what you were looking for?"

"I'll tell you all about it in the morning."

"While we're driving out to Navoe."

She gave me a hard look. "For what, may I ask? I've never left anything there I wanted to go back for."

"Jessie. I left her there today."

She started to say something, then changed her mind.

"Yes?" I asked.

She stared at me for a full minute before she said, "Why bother?"

The *Oakalla Reporter* came out on Friday as scheduled. Late Friday morning I sat within my office, surveying the light-green cement walls, waiting for the phone to ring. As a reporter, I knew when I had a story, and this week I didn't. As an editor, I knew when an edition stunk, and this one did. As a publisher, I knew I should fire myself. I didn't have time to play detective and print a newspaper.

The printer came into my office. He was reading a copy of the *Reporter*. "Save your eyes," I said.

"I was just looking for that article on Si Buckles. We *did* run it, didn't we?"

The phone rang. I answered it. "Garth Ryland here."

"I missed Si Buckles this week. Why?"

"I'm still working on the ending."

"Be a shame to leave us hanging in midair."

"I understand that, Mrs. Carrington."

"I hoped you did." She hung up.

"Mrs. Carrington?" the printer asked.

"One of our advertisers."

"She missed the article on Si Buckles, too, huh?"

I nodded.

"It was a good article. Maybe your best. Old Si, well, I never saw him in his true light before. I always thought his jokes were sort of harmless, and they are . . . until you start adding them up. What it amounts to then is a lot of hurt to a lot of people."

The phone rang again. "Garth Ryland here."

"Garth! How are you?"

"Fine, Truman."

"I thought you might be under the weather. Maybe had a new boy writing this week?"

"No, it's all mine."

"Busy week, huh? A lot going on?"

"Yeah, it was a busy week."

"You're still working on Si Buckles, aren't you?"

"Yes. I'm still working on him."

"Good! That's all I wanted to know." He hung up.

"Another one of our advertisers?" the printer asked.

"Our biggest."

"Seems you've got everyone's attention."

"It seems like it."

"You know what the problem is? Expectations. A sinner does one good deed and he's a shoo-in for sainthood. A saint makes one slip-up, and he's hellfired and damnationed. You can't promise what you don't deliver."

"May I quote you next edition?"

"Just make sure you spell my name right." He looked out the window. "You better circle the wagons, you've got lots of company coming. I think I'll go out the back door."

"I'll go with you."

"Isn't that desertion?"

"It's been called that."

I walked home, got Jessie, and retraced the route we'd driven the day of Phil's funeral. The name Wyandotte still stuck in my mind like a lump of peanut butter, and I thought a trip out there might help clear the air. I glanced at the sky. A north wind had come up, bringing clouds with it, and the sun kept peeping in and out of sight. It felt good when the sun was out, but it was damned cold when it wasn't. A not-too-original philosopher might say that life was a partly cloudy day and leave it to posterity to figure out just what the hell he meant—if anything. I found that most philosophers were most profound when they didn't try to explain themselves.

I thought I heard Jessie cough ominously as I stopped at the ruins of Wyandotte. Even yet I remembered the house was orange brick and that it shown with a strange luster in the moonlight that made the hair on my neck tingle and the adrenaline pump all the way down to my socks. Phosphorescent. It had that kind of glow, like the translucent sides of a pumpkin when a candle burns within.

As a special lady once told me in an airport on the eve of her departure, the inevitable can't be postponed forever. I got out of Jessie and started walking. When I found the first orange brick, I knew I'd come to the right place. A short way ahead I found the rest of the house, lying in a black and orange pile. Black and orange? Halloween! Something clicked in my mind like the first tumbler of a lock, but I couldn't take it any further.

I searched the area, finding only more bricks. I'd started back toward Jessie when I saw some initials carved on a beech. I moved closer and read them. R.C. + D.C. They'd been there a long time, but I had no way of knowing how long. Glancing down, I saw a knife wedged between the roots of the beech. I worked the knife loose and examined it. It was a Boy Scout knife, rusted almost beyond recognition. I cleaned it off as best I could on my shirt. There were some markings scratched on it, but I couldn't read them. I looked again at the initials on the tree: R.C. + D.C. I wondered.

I drove to Navoe Cemetery, as a huge cloud flattened into a grey anvil and spread across the sky, taking the sun with it. But I was in luck. Ruben stood beside Phil Chesterson's grave, his back to the wind, his body rock steady as though he were planted there. When he turned to face me, his eyes had the watery look of a sailor gazing out to sea.

I reached into my pocket and took out the knife, handing it to him. "Is this yours?"

He studied it. "Yes. I lost it the other day when I was digging sassafras. Where did you find it?"

"Wyandotte."

He cocked his head like a robin listening for a worm. "Are you sure? I don't remember being there."

"Where were you digging sassafras?"

"Just down the road." He handed the knife back to me. "I guess it can't be mine then."

"Could you have found it and lost it again?"

He was confused. "I'd remember, wouldn't I?"

"Not if something happened in the meantime."

His smile widened. "Nothing ever happens to me, Mr. Ryland. You know that."

"Maybe a long time ago?"

"I'm sorry, Mr. Ryland. I can't remember."

"Diana Chesterson—do you ever remember carving her initials on a beech?"

"I might have. You're not sore about it, are you?"

"No, Ruben. I've felt like doing it myself a time or two." The wind was growing colder, and the sky was now completely overcast. I looked across Navoe Cemetery, at the rows of white markers, then back to Ruben. I wondered how he stood it. "I'd better be going."

"Me, too, Mr. Ryland."

But he was still standing there when I drove away.

I met Tillie at the entrance to Broken Claw where she flagged me down. "Need a ride?" I asked.

"Nope."

I opened the door for her. "At least get inside out of the cold."

"How do I know I can trust you?"

"You don't."

She climbed in beside me. "What the hell."

"What's on your mind?"

She pulled her sweater tighter around her. "I saw him."

—— 94 ——

"Who?"

"Si Buckles."

"When?"

"Last night."

"You're sure?"

"Sure as I'm sitting here. You ever seen foxfire? Well, that's what I saw standing beside Si Buckles' grave. Only it wasn't foxfire. It was a man."

"How do you know it was Si Buckles?"

"I know, that's all. If I wasn't sure, I wouldn't have flagged you down."

"Where did he go from there?"

"Back into his grave for all I know. The moon came out from under a cloud, and I lost sight of him."

"You mean went under a cloud, don't you?"

"I mean came out from under a cloud. It was pitch dark when I saw him standing there." She opened the door. "There's one more thing. I didn't tell no one else before because they think I'm crazy enough the way it is. I'm not sure why I'm telling you now. But the night of the snowstorm I saw Santa Claus walking down the road through the snow."

"Santa Claus?"

She started to get out. "I knew you wouldn't believe me."

"Now, wait a minute." I reached across her, closing the door. "How do you know it was Santa Claus? Was it his hat? His beard? His reindeer? What?"

"His sack. He was carrying a sack."

"Going toward town?"

"Right."

"Did he leave you anything?"

"Not that I know of."

"Maybe his elves are on strike."

"I considered that possibility." She smiled shrewdly at me. "But I guess we'll never know, will we?"

I glanced at the water beneath Broken Claw where a hidden boulder sprouted a white plume. Today I could believe anything. "Speaking of stories, is it true what they say about this bridge, that you can see a hand reaching from the water when the moon's full?"

"I did once." Her face was deadpan, not even a hint of a smile.

"When was that?"

"Right after I drank a pint of blackberry brandy. You'd be surprised at all I saw that night."

"I imagine I would." I saw her hand on the door handle. "You sure I can't take you home?"

"Nope. My roof's in sight. By the time you got turned around, I'll be there." She closed one eye and studied me. "It's getting to you, ain't it, trying to make sense out of all this?"

"It's getting to me."

She climbed out of the car. "I thought so."

"Tillie, are you sure it was Santa Claus?"

"I didn't say for sure. I only said it looked like him." She slammed the door and began walking.

At home Ruth waited for me at the door. I could see I was in trouble. She had the same look my mother always had when I'd come home late from the creek. It was that "I'll kill you if you're not already dead" look.

I took the offensive and led her inside. "You still have your magnifying glass?" I asked.

She glanced sharply at me. She knew she wanted to tell me something, but at the moment it eluded her. "Somewhere in here. Let me go look." I went into the kitchen and turned on the light. She returned a few minutes later. "Here it is."

I examined the scratches on the knife. "Okay, now you take a look and tell me what you see."

She waved the magnifying glass in front of her eyes. "Rust."

"Astute."

"Well, what am I supposed to see? Wait a minute! I see it

now! It's white with a pink shell. Kind of a cute little thing."

I reached for the glass. "Forget it."

"The initials are R.C., is that what you wanted to know?"

"That's what I wanted to know."

"Where did you find it?"

"Wyandotte. Does that ring a bell?"

"Sure. Everybody around here knows about Wyandotte."

"Why?"

"That's where the Hull House was. Most people thought it was haunted."

"But you didn't?"

"I don't believe in ghosts."

"Neither do I, but lately I've been wondering. When did the Hull House burn?"

"Twenty years or so ago. The walls stood awhile longer, but they finally caved in."

"How did it burn?"

"No one knows. Since it was abandoned, no one bothered to find out." She looked at the stove. "Speaking of burning, that's what happened to your supper."

"A little charcoal never hurt anybody."

"You could grill steaks on this. Tuna casserole a la brick."

"I'll get something at the Corner." I picked up a copy of the *Oakalla Reporter*. "Any phone calls today?" I made the mistake of asking.

She smacked her fist against her head. "*That's* why I met you at the door! I've answered the phone so many times today I've got tennis elbow! And all of them wanting to know where Si Buckles was. I didn't know where he was, but I suggested where they might put him once they found him."

"How many are suing for damages?"

"Eight, by my last count."

The Corner Bar and Grill was nearly empty. With my choice of seats, I took the booth in the far corner away from the door. I ordered a shrimp basket with tossed salad and listened to them playing euchre in the back room. The lone patron at the bar was reading the *Oakalla Reporter*. At any moment I expected him to stand, mash it into a ball, and throw it at me. When he didn't, I thought perhaps he was asleep.

"Garth?" he finally said.

"Yes, Robbie?"

"This paper stinks."

"I agree."

"Now, I don't have anything against 'The Beauty of Spring,' but I was hoping for Si Buckles. You know what I mean?"

"I think so."

"At least you could have mentioned my name."

"What did he do to you?"

"It happened about eight years ago. My wife went out of town one weekend to visit her mother, and I left town to go fishing. While we were gone, somebody sneaked into our house and put a woman's stockings and pants and bra right where my wife would be sure to find them. She did all right. She filed for divorce the next day."

"She go through with it?"

"Took me for everything I had. For ten years I was a faithful husband. Then overnight I lost my job, home, car, wife, and two kids. It makes you wonder, doesn't it?"

It made me wonder because I hadn't read anything about it in the diaries. "You sure it was Si?"

"Who else? It had to be him or Doc."

"Eight years ago, you say?"

"Eight years ago this July."

"If I find it, I'll try to mention it next edition. . . . If that'll help any?"

He slid from the bar stool and landed heavily on the floor. It wasn't the first time I'd seen Robbie Davis drunk. It probably wouldn't be the last. "It won't do no good. She's married again for the third time. Still I know where she's living now. I'd kind of like to set the record straight."

The shrimp came, and I ordered a beer to drink with them. The beer helped make the room seem less empty than it was. I tried, but couldn't shake the memory of the house at Wyandotte. I could still see its orange brick glowing in the moonlight, while its windows glared like the eyes of a jack-o'-lantern. I wished I could make the connection now swirling in my mind.

Fran entered the bar by the side door, took one look around, and came directly to my table. He was gaunt and pale, his face unshaven, his clothes rumpled like those of a tramp. The bartender started over, but Fran waved him away. "Nothing tonight, Hiram."

"Fran, you're killing yourself," I said.

He smiled, rubbing the stubble on his chin. "That would be convenient, wouldn't it?" He leaned forward, his eyes red and swollen. "I came home early last night. Your car was there, but I didn't see you or Diana anywhere around."

"How early?"

"I don't remember."

"How early, Fran?"

"One, maybe two. I said I don't remember."

"At one I was printing a newspaper and Diana was in bed. At two I was still printing a newspaper and Diana was still in bed."

He leaned back and spread his arms over the top of the booth. "I might be wrong about the time."

"You're also wrong about what you're thinking. I'm not sleeping with her. I never have."

"Let's drop it, huh. I made a bluff and you called me on it. Go ahead and eat your supper."

I offered him a shrimp. "You want some? I've got plenty."

"I'm not hungry."

"You going home from here?"

—— 99 ——

"No, not yet."

"You need to go home."

He nodded at my plate. "Your shrimp's getting cold."

"Why don't you tell me what's got ahold of you?"

"Because it's none of your business."

"I'd like to help."

He laughed without humor. "You're forty years too late. You've heard of a self-made man? Well, I'm a self-made fool." He stood, preparing to leave. "Enjoy your supper."

"The last laugh."

He seemed to rock backwards as if I'd struck him. "What did you say?"

"That's it, isn't it? The last laugh—that's what's eating you alive?"

"Just how much do you know?"

"You're the gambler. Call my bluff."

He smiled. It was a bitter, hopeless smile. "I'm sorry, my friend. I don't feel lucky." He walked to the door, holding it a moment before he let it swing shut behind him.

I sat for a while staring at the shrimp, then pushed them aside. "Something wrong?" the bartender asked.

"Not with the shrimp, no."

"I told Helen to change the grease."

"They're fine, Hiram."

I rose, paid for my supper, and walked outside. The wind was still blowing hard, the tree branches clicking like castanets, and it was spitting snow. Jamming my hands into my pockets, I faced the wind. A hell of a night for April.

Diana was still up. She wore a thin, cotton robe, and her hair was wet and freshly washed. I stood a moment in the doorway staring at her. I knew why I'd come. There are certain stops you have to make in your life when you touch base with a soulmate. And for someone who'd been around as much as I, the chance didn't come that often.

"You look tired," she said.

"I am."

"I'll be right back." While I waited, I studied the utility

room. Its walls were covered with yellow poplar boards from an old sugar camp; a dry sink holding a pitcher and bowl sat in one corner, and a single tree hung above the door. Except for the appliances, everything in the room was older than I was. I hoped I'd hold up as well. "Come here, you." She led me into the family room where she put her feather pillow from her bed on her lap and me on the pillow. I kissed her fingers. There was magic in them, a magic I'd found nowhere else. I felt myself relaxing, as the tension of the past few days began to flow from me through her.

She smoothed my hair. "I can't really tell," she said.

"What's that?"

"Whether Fran saw you tonight?"

"He did."

"He confronted me today. It wasn't pleasant."

"What did you tell him?"

"I told him there was nothing between us."

"I told him the same thing."

"At least one of us lied."

"Yeah, at least one of us."

She leaned back, her hands resting on my chest. "I never thought I'd see the day when Fran Baldwin would need anyone's pity."

I didn't answer. I'd closed my eyes and was nearly asleep.

"Go ahead. I'll awaken you," she said.

"No, I don't dare. I can't stay."

"Why not?"

"Too many things to do."

"Can't they wait?"

"I wish they could." I stared at the ceiling. The house at Wyandotte kept coming back to me. "I took a drive today. You'll never guess what I saw carved on a beech tree."

"My initials?"

"Right. Can you guess who put them there?"

"Fran?"

"Ruben."

"*Ruben*. Are you sure?"

"Yes. It must've been years ago."

Her voice softened, "At Wyandotte you say?"

I looked up at her. "No, I didn't say. But that's where they are. How'd you know?"

Her eyes never wavered. "I must've read your mind. Garth, I'd like to see them sometime."

"First chance we'll go out there."

"How about tomorrow?"

"I'll have to see how tomorrow goes."

"Then I might go myself."

"That's up to you." I glanced around the room. I saw a copy of the *Reporter* lying on the coffee table. I knew I shouldn't ask, but I did anyway. "Well, what did you think of my column today?"

She laughed. "'The Beauty of Spring'? I almost gagged on it. I didn't know you knew so many clichés."

"Did you ever stop to think it might have been a parody?"

"If it was, it was perfect." Her eyes skewered me. "Was it?"

"I'll never tell." I sat up. "Thanks for the pillow. May I take it home with me?"

"Only if I can come along."

I handed it back to her. "Not tonight."

"Garth, why the 'Beauty of Spring' bit? Whom are you protecting, Fran or me?"

"I just didn't have a feature this week, that's all."

"I know better. There's enough in those diaries to fill a book. I repeat, whom are you protecting, Fran or me? If it's me, I don't want it. I've had that kind of protection all my life. It's demeaning when you really think about it."

"I haven't really thought about it. Good night, Diana."

Outside, the clouds had begun to roll back, leaving one narrow pane of sky. Within it the stars were sprinkled like broken glass, some large and bold, others the point of a sliver. I thought about what Diana had said. I didn't know the answer. In this era of the emancipated woman and the enlightened man, I was as much of a throwback as Emily Post. I still let women open doors for me, light their own cigarettes, and pick up the tab if I was running short that day. And they could still invite me into their factory, their office, and their bed without losing my respect. But when it came to war or danger or death, I wanted to be the one who went in first and came out last. If that made me a macho, fascist, sexist pig, then I guessed I was.

The now familiar light was on in the basement of the mortuary. I hesitated before I went inside. I had the same love of basements as I did of tunnels. Besides, this one smelled of Formalin. It made me think of death.

Fran was sitting at the card table reading a magazine. He looked up, nodded, then returned to the magazine. "How long does this go on?" I asked.

He looked at his watch. "Four more hours."

"Then that's it?"

"That's it for tonight."

"Why *here*? Why are you waiting here?"

"That's where Phil saw him."

"Saw *whom*?"

He didn't answer, but pointed to a gap in the bushes outside. "He came right through there. Wait a minute." He got up and turned off the basement light. "You can see better this way."

"Turn it back on."

"What's the matter, you're not afraid of the dark, are you?" He laughed, turning the light back on.

I picked up the magazine he was reading. It was a copy of *Beyond Reality*. I threw it down. "Nothing to eat, no sleep, and now *this*. What are you trying to do to yourself?"

"Scare myself to death, what else?"

"That's insane!"

"Of course, it's insane. That's why I'm doing it."

"Fran, whatever your reason, it's not worth it!"

His eyes were two bright coals, as if fanned by a sudden draft. "My peace of mind isn't worth it? Take my word, nobody knows better than I what I'm doing to myself. All truth is a form of madness. It has its seekers and its zealots and its martyrs. But when it's over, I'll *know*. God help me, I'll *know*."

"Know what?"

He smiled at me, his eyes opaque. "If Si Buckles *lives*."

"For Christ's sake, Fran! Si Buckles is dead!"

"Is he? How do you know? Did fate single out you alone for omniscience? You're an intelligent man, Garth, one of the brightest I've had the pleasure to know, but you can't even begin to touch all the mysteries of the universe. Man as a race has just begun, and now the more certain he is of his world, the less certain he is of his own mind. You explain it, Garth. How did a man with my promise end up in the basement of a mortuary watching for a ghost?"

"By his own choice."

"That's a convenient answer."

"That's the truth."

"You seem certain. I wonder how certain you'll be a year, or even a week from now?"

"You won't go home, and you won't let me stay?"

"No."

"Then how can you say it's not your own choice?"

He picked up the magazine and began to read. "Good night, Garth."

"Fran, sometimes you need help. Sometimes you have to say uncle."

"Good night, Garth."

I was outside on the basement steps when the basement light went out. I stood a moment, surveying the tangled bushes, the gap through which Si Buckles had come. Tonight, the wind in the trees, the clouds in dark convolutions, it seemed possible.

C H A P T E R   8

I awakened long before dawn. I wasn't sure I even slept, but rolled from one side of the bed to the other so many times I was seasick. I closed my eyes and tried to picture a hammock gently swaying in a summer breeze. Instead, I thought of Wyandotte, and that was the end of that.

I got up and walked across the hall to my study. I counted the diaries. Twenty-four in all. Twenty-four years of a man's life and all he had to show for it was a few laughs. A waste? Who'd ever know? Maybe Si Buckles went as far as he could go.

Ruth came down the hall and looked in at me. "It's you. Good. I'm going back to bed."

"Why don't you keep me company for a while?"

"Garth, it's the middle of the night!"

"Long enough for a question or two?"

She sighed, sitting on the floor beside me. "Okay, what do you want to know?"

"What about Si Buckles' family?"

"What about them?"

"Any brothers or sisters?"

"No. After they had him, his parents gave up."

"Any first cousins?"

"A couple. They live out of state."

"Do they resemble him in any way?"

"God help them if they do. They're both women. What are you getting at?"

"I'm drawing a profile of Si Buckles."

"Any blank circle will do."

"What about his friends?"

"Two. Phil Chesterson and Fran Baldwin—if you want to call them that."

"How about when he was a boy?"

"One. Ruben Coalman. That lasted until about the time Si moved here."

"When was that?"

"When they were eleven or twelve. I don't know exactly."

"Ruben and Si were the same age, right?"

"Close. They were at most a year apart."

"Why did they stop being friends?"

"You know how kids are. They outgrow each other just like they do their clothes. By the time he was ten, Ruben was already smarter than Si ever would be. In a way it was a shame, too. He was the only real friend Si ever had."

"Where did Si live before he moved here?"

"The mortuary. His mother had a second-floor apartment there."

"With an outside entrance?"

"Yeah, there's a back stairs."

"What's in there now, do you know?"

"Nothing that I know of. Phil only used the first floor and the basement. He sealed the rest of it off."

"Why didn't he use it to live in?"

"He said he couldn't sleep with a body in the house. I can't say that I blame him." She yawned. "Speaking of sleeping, that's becoming a lost art around here. So if you'll excuse me . . ."

"Ruth, what's in our attic?"

"Cobwebs and rafters. Why?"

"If Si used to live here, some of his stuff might still be around."

"Have a look for yourself. I'm going back to bed."

I looked in the attic. She was right—cobwebs and rafters and spiders.

At daybreak I parked in Si Buckles' driveway. Stepping from Jessie, I could see my breath roll from my mouth. I patted her fenders. She didn't like cold weather at all. There must've been an M.G. hanging somewhere on her family tree.

Taking a flashlight from the glove compartment, I went inside the house. The must had thickened in the cold, and the faint smell of smoke still lingered. The house itself seemed frozen the way Si had left it. I felt an intruder, the way I did whenever I visited Indian ruins, as though the Great Hopi were frowning down on me.

I searched the house, but didn't find anything new. Entering the garage, I found the opening to the attic in the ceiling. As I followed the flashlight's dusty beam around the perimeter of the attic, I learned two things: There was nothing here; I needed new batteries. I folded Si's step ladder and put it back into place. It was stiff and new. I doubted it had ever been used. I looked around the garage. Everything in it was new, including his Volkswagen. How could a man live forty years and not leave his imprint on anything? If I valued my sanity, I'd have to leave that question to the Muses. I climbed into Jessie and turned the key. She sputtered, but finally fired. I took that as a warning of things to come.

The hardware was now open, and Fritz Gascho, the owner, was stocking his shelves. It was the local hangout of the old men of the town, and in winter they gathered around its wood-burning stove and swapped stories and made the hot iron hiss with their tobacco juice. It was an old store, the oldest in Oakalla, with soft wooden floors, a mahogany staircase, and a huge black fan that turned lazily overhead like a summer windmill. Even on its busiest days, its pace was always mellow, and I liked to go there and just stand, soaking up a part of me and my past that would never be again.

Fritz stopped when he saw me and came out from behind the counter to shake my hand. "Morning, Garth. What can I do for you?"

"I've been wondering, how long did Si Buckles work here?"

"Twenty-two years. He started the day after he graduated from high school and never missed a day until he died."

"How well did you know him?"

"Not as well as I do now, thanks to you. It's funny how you can work alongside a man all those years and not know what's going through his head. It makes you wonder about yourself, how well anyone really knows you."

"You seem to have some question about it?"

"Nothing I can really put my finger on. I know Si'd do about anything for a joke, but I didn't think there was a mean bone in his body. If there was, he didn't know it. I guess what I'm saying is that he never intended to hurt anybody, the way it sounds in your newspaper."

"The words are his, not mine."

"Yeah, that's what bothers me. If it hadn't come from Si's own mouth, I wouldn't believe it."

"Did he ever tell you about his illness, that he was dying?"

"As a matter of fact, he did. He was acting down one day, and I asked him what was wrong and that's when he told me. It sure surprised me. He looked as healthy as a horse."

"Did he tell anyone else?"

"Not that I know of. Neither did I, in case you're wondering."

"Do you remember most of the jokes he pulled?"

"I remember some of them."

"Did he ever mention the last laugh to you?"

"No, I can't say he did. Is it important?"

"I don't know, Fritz. It seems to be." I looked around the store. It was snug, comfortable, like bourbon and an overstuffed chair. "Any more break-ins lately?" I asked.

"No."

"Has anything turned up missing?"

"Only a roll of tinfoil. I remember because I left it setting next to the paint, and I was planning to put it back."

"Why would anyone want tinfoil enough to steal it?"

"I figure it's kids. Some of them will do anything on a dare. Then, of course, I might have misplaced it."

"Well, if anything else turns up missing, let me know, will you?"

"You can count on it."

My next stop was the Five and Dime, Oakalla's second-oldest store, which along with the bank next door had had a recent face-lifting. Over the years I'd seen its owner Harold Weaver go from a fair-haired Jaycee to a bent old man crippled with arthritis. In a way he symbolized the fate of the Five and Dime, which every year lost more of its customers to Woolco and K-Mart and the rest of the chains that sprang up like weeds through the cracks of suburbia. But he'd never lost his sense of humor. And his store still had the warmth of country about it. No piped-in music, no Bargain Mouth on the loudspeaker, no Miss Anonymous at the cash register. Just Harold puttering about his failing store and looking contented.

"Find what you're looking for, Garth?" he finally asked.

"I think so." I'd picked up a diary that looked very much like the ones I had at home. "I see Si Buckles shopped here."

He moved in for a closer look. "No, can't say he did. Not on a regular basis anyway. He got most of what he needed over at the hardware. Discount, you see. For working there."

"But he did make it in at least once a year?"

Harold's eyes twinkled with humor. "Twice, as I recall.

Bought a loaf of bread and a roll of toilet paper each time. No diaries, though, if that's what you're asking."

"You're sure? This one looks like a perfect match for one I have at home."

"Probably is for all I know. But he didn't buy it here. Might have stolen it, though. You can't rule that out."

"What makes you say that?"

"As long as I knew him, and that was all his life, Si never left town to do his shopping. Fact is he hardly ever left town period. So since I'm the only one in town that stocks these and since Si never bought them out of town and never bought them here, how did he end up with them unless he stole them?"

"Somebody else could've bought them for him."

"Don't know who. Do you?"

"Not at the moment."

He rubbed his chin and winced, as if any action hurt his arthritic fingers. "Except Si never struck me as a thief, or a liar either for that matter. That's what gets me to wondering about those diaries. In a couple of instances he sure got his facts all mixed up. Or was that you taking poetic license?"

"As I told Fritz, the words are Si's, not mine."

"Well, he sure told a good story anyway. A lot better one than I'd expect out of Si. Just goes to show you, doesn't it?"

"Show you what?"

"I was hoping you'd tell me."

I thanked him and left.

Jessie wouldn't start—no matter how tenderly I cursed her—so I walked to the mortuary. It looked different in daylight without the wind whistling through its vines and my imagination running wild. Actually, it was a stately old home, and might have been attractive with a little better care and some shutters and trim. Never beautiful, though. It was too stern, too massive. And, daylight or dark, too damn stark for my taste.

I knocked at the front door. No one answered. I didn't

expect anyone since Maryanne had officially closed the mortuary after Phil died. I walked around back and found the stairs Ruth had told me about. It was an easy climb to the top, and the door there was unlocked. I pushed on it, and it gave easily, almost as though I were expected. Checking the door more closely, I discovered the lock had literally been ripped off. Whoever had done the hatchet job was either in a big hurry or he didn't like locked doors.

Inside, it was cool and damp, not yet warmed by the sun. Stepping over a strip of torn wallpaper, I entered a narrow hall where native two-by-fours showed like ribs through the holes in the plaster. I went from room to room, stopping at each to survey the contents and to blow in my hands to get the blood moving again. Either the rooms were built for boarders to squeeze every nickel out of every square inch or Snow White and her entourage had their winter quarters here. They were all cramped, bare, and cold enough to raise goose bumps on the brass doorknobs.

The room at the far end of the hall, though, was somehow different from the others. I didn't know why until I made the association with the mud on the floor and the stained lace curtain covering the window. It looked lived in, that someone had stayed here recently. There was one other difference. It was a hell of a lot warmer than the other rooms.

I felt the register. It was cold. I opened the curtain and looked out. The sun was on the other side of the house. So where did the heat come from? Returning to the register, I felt inside the duct. The air here was warmer than in the room. Evidently this was one duct Phil forgot to close when he sealed the upstairs. Picking up a piece of mud, I stared at it a moment. It wasn't mud. It was clay—blue clay. Then I dropped it into the duct and listened as it rattled all the way down to the basement. The duct had to be open.

Before I left, I took another look around the room. It still seemed lived in. There were fewer spider webs than in the other rooms, and the dust was stirred into uneven piles. Opening the closet door, I saw something that made me wish I wasn't so nosy. Carved on the wall of the closet were the initials S.B., and beneath them was the remnant of what had once been a baseball card. I picked up the card. Bob Feller. The more I thought, the more certain I was that this was Si Buckles' old bedroom.

Outside, the sun was more than welcome, as I walked slowly down the stairs and onto the walk that led to the basement. I went inside where the furnace was running with a steady hum. I checked the network of hot-air ducts, and everything seemed in order. Then the furnace stopped, as the quiet settled in. Reaching for the light cord, I saw the register in the ceiling directly above the card table. I wondered. I just wondered . . .

"Garth Ryland, I've pulled some crazy stunts in my day, but this tops them all!" I'd gone to get Ruth and she now sat at the card table in the basement of the mortuary. "What if somebody comes in?"

I handed her a deck of cards. "Ask them if they'd like to play."

"What if they say no?"

"Ask them if they'd like to watch."

"And where will you be?"

"Around."

"You're not leaving me here?"

"I'll be close enough to hear you scream."

I went around back, climbed the stairs, and reentered the room at the end of the hall. With my ear pressed to the register, I could hear the cards hit the table and Ruth mumbling to herself. "Who's winning?" I asked her through the register.

"Who wants to know?"

"Si Buckles."

There was a long pause. "Garth Ryland, where are

you?" I laughed my deepest, most sinister laugh. "That's it! The party's over!"

"Ruth, I'm upstairs."

"*Where* upstairs?"

"Second floor."

"I'd swear you were down here with me."

"Do me a favor. Walk over by the door." I gave her time to do it. "Can you hear me now?"

"Barely."

"Same here. Try someplace else." She moved to several places around the basement. None was as clear as when she sat at the card table.

"What's that I smell anyway?"

"Probably embalming fluid." There was another pause. "Are you all right?" I asked.

"No. I just remembered where I was. Are you through playing games?"

"I'll be down in a minute. Wait for me there."

"I'll wait for you outside." She was waiting in her car when I got downstairs. "Okay, so what does all this prove?" she asked as I climbed in beside her.

"Nothing."

"You brought me over here for nothing?"

"I wondered if you could hear a conversation in the basement from where I was on the second floor."

"Where were you on the second floor?"

"I think it was Si's old bedroom."

"I'm sorry I asked. What were you doing there in the first place?"

"Looking for ghosts."

"You find any?"

"No. All I found was this." I handed her the baseball card.

She held it up where she could read it. "I forgot. He used to collect them. It was the only hobby he ever had." She carefully put it into her pocket so she wouldn't tear it. I wondered if she hated Si as much as she let on. "He gave it up about the same time he and Ruben parted ways." She studied me closely. "What are you thinking?"

"Nothing that makes sense right now. Did you have any luck with the diaries?"

"No. And I've had about all I can take for one day."

"I'll take over from here."

I went home and began reading diaries. I was still there the next morning when the phone rang.

"**G**arth . . . ?"

"Diana, what's wrong?"

"It's Fran . . . he's dead. I heard a shot. I went into the kitchen . . ."

"Have you called Sheriff Roberts?"

"No."

"Do."

"He's *dead*, Garth. Garth . . . he's *dead*." She was starting to come apart.

"Hang on until I get there." I went to the garage and raised the door. It took me a moment to realize Jessie was still uptown. "Damn."

I didn't remember getting there, whether I walked or ran or what. It seemed I left my garage and came in her front door. Diana hit me a ton. I thought we were both going over. Then she began to shake, and the tighter I held her, the more she shook until she had us both shaking. At last she began to cry, and it was better. I took her into the family room, wrapped her in an afghan, and set her in an overstuffed chair. "Don't move until I come back," I said. She closed her eyes and nodded.

Fran was dead. I didn't need a coroner to tell me that. As a correspondent, I'd been in Vietnam when it was supposedly still a land of friendly farmers, and the only thing we shipped from there was bullshit and rice. And a few bodies that nobody counted, except those of us who'd watched them die. I said then I'd never get used to death, and I never had. I was one of the lucky ones. I got out before the bodies got too many to count. But I still knew death when I saw it.

I glanced around the kitchen. It looked the same as always—cozy, clean, everything in its place. What blood there was lay drying on the table and could still be erased with one swipe of a sponge. Only one small, neat hole in Fran's right temple made the difference between this and any other morning. I looked at him for a long time, wanting to shake him back to life, to see his arrogant smile tell me this was all a joke. I clasped his shoulder. "Jesus Christ, Fran!"

The doorbell rang. I answered it. "Come in, Rupert. He's in the kitchen," I said.

"I'd been here sooner, but . . ." He saw Diana huddled in the chair. "I'll tell you later." We went into the kitchen where he examined Fran. He shook his head and sighed. "It doesn't get easier, Garth. Never let anybody tell you it does." Using a pencil, he picked up the revolver lying beside Fran on the floor. "Look at these shells. They're so old they're corroded. It's a wonder it ever fired." He nodded toward the family room. "Do you think she's up to answering some questions?"

"I think so."

"I'll be as gentle as I can."

We went into the family room where Diana sat gazing at Fran's favorite chair. "Good morning, Sheriff," she said, turning to us.

"Morning, Mrs. Baldwin. Do you feel like telling me what happened?"

"I'm not feeling right now, so it really doesn't matter."

"You mind if I sit down?" he asked.

"I'm sorry. I should have . . ." She looked away.

"It's okay," he said.

I brought him a chair, then checked with Diana. "Are you going to be all right?"

"I'll be fine."

"We can do this later, Mrs. Baldwin," Rupert said.

"No. I'd like to get it over with now."

He opened his note pad. "When did you last see your husband alive?"

"Earlier this morning. Around four, I think."

"He'd been out all night?"

"Yes."

"Do you know where?"

"The basement of the mortuary."

"What the hell was he doing there?"

"Waiting for Si Buckles," I answered.

He took off his hat and set it on the floor. "You know I can't write that down. They'd have us all in the first padded truck going north." He sighed. "Let me see. Visiting an old friend! That ought to do it. Now, Mrs. Baldwin, did Dr. Baldwin speak to you when he came in?"

"No. He kissed me and then slumped against the bed. I don't know if he was holding me or I was holding him."

"Then he got up?"

"Not for a long time. It seemed like a long time anyway. I was in and out of sleep, and he kept floating in and out of my dreams. Finally, he said he was going down and make coffee. I told him I would, but he said no. He kissed me again and . . ." Her hands tightened on the chair. "You know the rest."

"Where did he keep his revolver?"

"I really don't know. I've never had much use for guns. He knew I didn't like having them around."

He closed his note pad. "That's enough for now." He stood, putting the chair back into place. "I'm going to have them do an autopsy, Mrs. Baldwin. Not because I don't believe you, but because I do. It'll clear the air once and for all."

"Thank you, Sheriff."

"I'm sorry, Mrs. Baldwin, for your sake. It's a damn shame."

"Yes, it is, isn't it, a man with his talent?" She rose and set the afghan aside. "Do you mind, Sheriff, if I spend a moment alone with him before you take him away? I know he can't hear me, but I'd like to say good-bye."

"We'll be outside."

I followed him outside into the backyard and together we watched the sunrise. It was peaceful there. The trees were wet and shining, and a wren bounced from limb to limb, spattering dew like welding sparks. "You know, it doesn't figure," Rupert said, "how a man with everything can end up with nothing. It's the great mystery of my life." He stared at the orange-striped sunrise. "There's no reason for it, not with a woman like that at home. The sonofabitch had to be crazy."

"Or thought he was."

"That's what I wanted to ask you. What the hell's going on around here? Guess where I was earlier this morning. Me and the menagerie—the cats rubbing at my ankles and the dogs sniffing at my pants and Tillie raving like a wild woman about Si Buckles rising up from the grave! I think me and the pig were the only sane ones there. It's starting to get to me, this Si Buckles thing! And if I remember right, you and those diaries are the ones that got the whole thing started." Out front, Operation Lifeline skidded to a stop, narrowly missing a tree. "Wait a minute. I'll get back to you." He walked to the ambulance, where three young attendants were hurriedly unloading a stretcher. "When it takes you over an hour to get here," he began, "there's no need to trip over yourselves getting into the house. Besides, it's too late anyway. The man's dead. So where have you been all this time?"

"We took a wrong turn. We don't know this end of the county very well. Mr. Chesterson always handled it before."

"Might I suggest you learn it. And one other suggestion:

Wait until the lady comes out before you go in. And . . ."
He paused for maximum effect, "if you slam this body
around like you did the last one, I'm going to shoot the
tires right off your new toy." He smiled at them, "That's
all." Then he returned to where I was standing. "I'd rather
ride in a log wagon with a broken leg than have them
turned loose on me. God save me from all volunteers.
Now, where were we?"

"You said Tillie saw Si Buckles again last night."

"Again?" His sallow face reddened. "Again! Why didn't
she report it the first time?"

"For the same reason you didn't write it down."

"Well, how far would I get with it?" He threw up his
hands. "Help me, Garth. I'm at a loss on this one. I don't
have the time, nor the inclination to stake out the
cemetery, but I don't know what else to do."

"I'll do what I can."

"You think you can solve it?"

"I have to."

"Why do you say that?"

"Diana. She's involved somehow. Don't ask me how I
know. It's a gut feeling that won't go away."

"Do you think she's next?"

"I'm afraid she might be."

Diana walked outside, as I went to her. Her face was
smudged with Fran's blood, and her hair strung down into
her eyes. Taking my hand, she stared at the eastern
horizon. "It's beautiful this morning, isn't it?" she said. "I'll
always remember it was a beautiful morning."

"Okay," Rupert said to the attendants, "you can go in
now. But remember what I said." He tipped his hat to
Diana. "I'm going now. If there's anything I can do, let me
know."

"I will. Thank you, Sheriff." She watched him leave,
then turned to me. "Do I look a mess?"

"It's not important."

"I was hysterical a minute ago. I couldn't let go of him. I

—— 119 ——

couldn't make myself." She smiled—it was a gentle, a lover's smile. "He looked so young, Garth, the way he did twenty years ago when I first gave my heart to him. It was as if death had released some terrible burden from him, and he was my Fran again—all dressed up in his padded sportscoat and white bucks ready to take me to my senior prom. You should have known him then, Garth. You'd have loved him, too. For all of his wonderful, wasted talent, he was still the most charming man I've ever known. I'll miss him. I'm just beginning to realize how much."

Phil's widow, Maryanne, parked along the curb and got out of her car. When she started running toward us, I heard Diana sob. I was no good at a time like this. I waited for Maryanne to reach us, then released Diana and went home.

Ruth was resting against the railing of the stairway. She had Si Buckles' chest full of diaries halfway down the stairs. I didn't know how she did it, but she could gather news faster than a telephone operator. "What are you doing?" I asked.

"What does it look like I'm doing? I'm getting ready to have a bonfire."

"Not with those, you're not."

"You just watch me. Remember I'm his next of kin." She glanced at the ceiling. "May God strike me dead if I ever repeat it."

"Ruth, I need those diaries."

"And I need a job. They won't pay me much for trimming around your gravestone."

"Nothing's going to happen to me."

"I know. I'm taking care of that right now." Instead, after a brief struggle, I took the chest from her and started up the stairs. "What do you hope to gain by it?" she asked.

"The answer's in here somewhere."

"If it is, I can't find it. I've been through them backwards and forwards so many times my eyes have warts. Si belonged a lot of places, but there's none better than where he is right now. So let's let him rest in peace."

"I'd like to."

"Then why don't you?"

"Because he won't let *me* rest in peace."

"Now, don't go talking like that." She took a step backwards.

"It's only a figure of speech."

"Talk around town is that he's been seen lately—as late as last night."

"By whom?"

"Somebody."

"That's what I thought. Si is dead, Ruth. That much I'm sure of."

"Well, I'm not anymore, and it's giving me the willies."

"What makes you say that?"

She straightened, ignoring my question. "Let me get my spine back in place and I'll fix you some breakfast."

"I'll get something later."

"How's Diana?" She seemed eager to talk about something else.

"She'll come through all right."

"Anybody there with her?"

"Maryanne is now."

"I'll stop by this afternoon."

"Tell her I'll be by later."

"Where are you going now?"

"For a drive in the country."

"You couldn't pick a better day."

"Yeah."

I walked uptown where Jessie still sat along the curb. I never worried about somebody stealing her. I didn't have that good of friends. She started on the first try, and a moment later I drove toward Navoe Cemetery, as the sun changed from red to gold, and wisps of clouds whitened like aging brows. Turning onto the gravel, I heard a meadowlark's trill, followed by the sharp click of a redwing blackbird. Some sounds you remember all of your life.

Tillie wasn't home, so I drove on to the cemetery. Ruben wasn't there, only the stones and the grass and the silence reserved for the dead. I walked to my grandmother's grave and waited for him, but after an hour I knew he wasn't coming. I wondered where he was. I'd forgotten this wasn't his home.

I met Tillie on the way back to town. She was carrying a small sack and had the determined look of a soldier marching. "Need a ride?" I asked.

"No, thanks. It's too pretty a day to be inside."

"Sheriff Roberts said you saw Si Buckles again."

"Yeah, and I meant to call, but when I saw him leave the cemetery and start up the road toward my place, my fingers dialed the first number they came to."

"What time was it, you remember?"

"One or after. That's when I usually let the dogs out and the cats in."

"What did the dogs do?"

"Nothing, not even a bark. They just sat on the porch and whined."

"Is that unusual?"

"Try walking this road sometime after dark and you'll see how unusual it is. Of course, they're getting to know you now. It might not be as bad."

"Where did he go after he left the cemetery?"

"Toward town."

"You're sure?"

"Well, I didn't ask him his itinerary, but that seemed the general direction he was heading."

"How long does it usually take you to walk into town?"

"A couple hours, if I hump it."

"Did you see him come back?"

"To tell you the truth, I wasn't looking. I was knee-deep in covers with my head buried like an ostrich." She shook the sack. "But I'll be ready for him next time. Bought me some quail loads. I figure that'll be about right for a ghost."

"What if you miss?"

"Hell, I ain't missed what I shot at in thirty years. I'm not about to start now."

"Can I have the pig if you do?"

"You can have the whole damn farm, pig and all." She thought a moment, scratching her chin. "Do you suppose I shouldn't fire until fired upon?"

"I wouldn't."

"You're probably right. Why make war at my age?" She waved and started on.

"Tillie, have you seen Ruben?"

"Nope. It ain't my day to watch him."

I watched her go, as her long dress fluttered in the breeze and the dust puffed from between her bare toes. She was an artist in her own right, not so much for what she did, but what she projected—the triumph of a free spirit.

Diana's house was filled with women, but I went in anyway. She came to me at once, taking my hand, as the house suddenly quieted. There were some knowing glances exchanged among the mourners, and when we stepped outside, things began to buzz within.

"Let them talk," she said. "It'll give them something to do." She led me into the backyard where we sat under a flowering redbud. "I really don't know why most of them came, whether they needed a good cry or somebody to talk to or what. I guess they feel it's their duty, that no one should mourn alone. I just wish they'd get out and go home." She sighed, picking a redbud petal from my hair. "I'm sorry, Garth. I'm not very good company today."

"You're not expected to be."

"Do you know what I wish? I wish I could laugh the way Fran used to when things got him down. He had such a mocking laugh—it made it all seem less real."

"It'll come in time."

"Do you think so? The way I feel now I'll never laugh again."

"How are you holding up otherwise?"

"Fine, I guess. I hear myself talking and find myself moving, so it must be me that's doing it." She straightened my collar. "Now, let's talk about something else—like where you went today? If ever I've needed you, it's now."

"I'm sorry. I didn't think I'd be missed."

"You know better. Why does death bother you so? Is it because you can't cry . . . or won't let yourself cry?"

"I can't explain it. I feel clumsy, that's all, that I'm just in the way. I say the wrong things, do the wrong things, laugh when I shouldn't . . . I've always been that way, even when I was a kid. Once I even went to the wrong funeral. It didn't matter. They're all the same."

"They serve their purpose."

"Yeah. Somebody once told me that."

"I'll bet you won't visit someone that you know is dying. I'll bet you wouldn't even visit me." Sometimes she was too perceptive for my own good.

"Let's talk about something else, huh. Like what Fran really did when he came home this morning?"

"I told you. We held each other for a while, and then he went to the kitchen to make coffee."

She was so damned beautiful sitting there beneath the redbud it was hard to believe she was lying. But she was. Something had happened to Fran last night to finally push him over the edge. I had to know what it was. "I don't believe you."

"Suit yourself."

"Diana, you might be in danger. Have you ever thought of that?"

"So might you. Have *you* ever thought of that?"

"I'm not involved. You are. This goes back long before my time."

"How can you be so sure?"

"Call it a gut reaction. A reporter lives and dies by them."

"If you're trying to reassure me, that's a poor choice of words. I've lost my husband and my brother and now why not you, right? Diana's a tough broad, she'll pull through okay. What's one more death among friends?" She started to cry. "Go ahead. Take off. I know it makes you nervous."

If there'd been so much as a gopher hole around I'd have tried to crawl into it. "I'm sorry."

"Well, then act like it."

I held her for a long time, long enough to watch each of her fellow mourners leave the house without a word. I wondered what they thought. Not that I cared. I'd been the talk of the town more than once in my life. But I hoped they understood—some of them anyway. If not, baby hadn't come as far as she thought she had.

"Shall we start over?" she asked, pulling away.

"I don't think we can."

"I don't mean us. I mean our conversation. The least I owe you is the truth."

"Did Fran see Si Buckles this morning? That's all I want to know."

"He saw something. He kept mumbling over and over, 'He's *alive*, Diana. He's *alive!*' I tried to get him to explain, but he wouldn't."

"Is anyone staying with you tonight?" I asked.

"Maryanne said she would."

I rose. "Good. I'll stop by in the morning."

"Where will you be tonight?"

"Nowhere for you to worry about."

"I can tell Maryanne not to bother."

"No. I'll be all right."

"I wasn't thinking of you this time. I was thinking of me—how good your arms will feel when the crash comes."

"I'll come by for a while."

"I'd appreciate it."

The first thing I did when I got home was call Rupert.

He was gone, but I finally tracked him down. He anticipated my question. "The little lady's in the clear, Garth. No question he shot himself and that was the gun he used. We checked it out, too. It's an antique, an old center fire twenty-two. It's registered in his name."

"Thanks, Rupert."

"I hated to do it, but like I told her, it'll clear the air once and for all."

"I'm sure she understands."

"You learn anything today?"

"Something about myself, that's all."

"Then it was a day well spent."

"I suppose. Thanks again."

"One favor, Garth. If you get in over your head, give me a call before it's too late."

"I plan to."

"See that you do."

The night following Fran's funeral the others had left, and Diana and I sat at opposite ends of the couch staring ahead at the bricks of the fireplace. After all the traffic of the past few days, the house seemed unnaturally quiet, the grandfather clock in the hall unusually loud. Taking off my shoes and socks, I dragged my feet through the burnt-orange carpet, thinking how good the grass would feel. I went to the window and opened it. It was warm outside, the air saturated with lilac bloom. "Would you like to take a walk?" I asked.

She kicked off her shoes. "Very much."

"We might get wet."

"I really don't mind."

I walked with my hands in my pockets and she with her hands in hers, as we made a wide circle of Oakalla. It had started to rain. Not hard. But large, intermittent drops that plopped as they hit. She threw her head back and let the rain wash her face. "It's funny, Garth," she said, stopping to squash some mud with her toes, "how fickle life is. At twenty all I could think of was getting married. From thirty on all I could think of was being free. Now, I'm free, and I don't feel a thing—not joy, not sorrow, not anticipation, not regret. It's a big fat nothing. I don't even know what I'm going to do with it."

She took her toes from the mud and left her footprint

neatly imbedded there. "And do you know what the kicker is? A child doesn't wonder. She's born free. She runs, laughs, falls, cries, then gets up again and goes right on as if nothing happened. Why do we have to relearn what once came naturally and unlearn all of the roles we've put ourselves in? What kind of logic's that?" I raised my arms in surrender. She smiled, her first in three days. "Well, it's a bitch, if you want to know the truth."

"I believe you. I've been there myself." It began to rain harder, slowly washing away her footprint. "Tell you what. I'll race you home. The winner gets a shoulder to cry on."

"Only if I get a head start." She was already taking one. "Okay, count three."

"One." She rolled up her pants legs. "Two." She began to jog. "Three!" She was a half block ahead of me and still gaining.

I took off on a half lope, half jog. I told myself I wasn't as intent on winning as I was on getting there. Then it really cut loose, and I couldn't see a damn thing but the rain. I ran harder. It was stupid, I knew; there was no way I could get any wetter. But Diana was somewhere ahead of me, and I at least wanted to keep it close. I was gaining on her. I could see her now. In two strides I was in position. With the third I tackled her, as we pitched headlong into a muddy lawn, plowing a furrow as we went. She got up sputtering, slipped, and knocked me backwards into a puddle. That started us laughing, and by the time we got back to her house, we couldn't even stand up. Falling on the kitchen floor, we laughed until it hurt and then laughed some more. Crawling to me, Diana rested her head on my muddy pants. "Thank you, Garth. I think I'll live now."

I scraped the mud from her face and wiped it on my shirt. "I'm not sure I will." I bent down and kissed her. "You sure you don't want me to stay the night?"

"I very much want you to stay. But I don't want to go from one man's keeping to another man's care."

I kissed her again. "Then I might as well start home. There are some things I have to do yet tonight."

"Si Buckles?"

"I've got Ruth reading his diaries. It's not exactly her favorite chore."

"It wouldn't be mine either. Call me in the morning?"

"As soon as I'm coherent."

I walked home in the rain. I hated to leave Diana alone, but she was right. You can't fly with one foot still on the ground. It was a balmy night, almost like summer, and I hardly felt the rain. Stopping along the sidewalk, I picked a blade of grass, positioned it between my palms, and blew. The squawk was long and loud. I smiled. Not bad for an old-timer.

At home Ruth was asleep in my study with one of the diaries in her lap. I sat down beside her and took the diary away. She opened her eyes. "What time is it anyway?"

"Eleven."

"That makes six hours and twenty-three minutes I've been up here. How time flies when you're having fun!"

"Find anything?"

"That's kind of hard to tell when you don't know what you're looking for."

"The last laugh. Anything that might point to it."

"To be honest, I don't really care at this point. I'm going to bed."

I took off my wet shirt. "Throw me my pillow and robe on your way, will you?"

"You're not sleeping here? God knows what might come creeping out of that chest!"

"I hope it's some answers."

She went on down the hall, while I opened the diary she'd been reading. It was Si Buckles' last diary, and if I remembered right, that given her choice, it was the one she always read. She was holding out on me. She wouldn't admit it, not even under oath, but there was something she knew about Si that she didn't want anyone else to know.

I listened to the rain on the roof. It had a numbing effect, like the slow plunk of a bass fiddle. I felt myself drifting, caught between the rain and my need for sleep. The phone rang.

"Do you want me to get it?" Ruth asked from her bedroom.

But I was already on my way downstairs. I'd had an uneasy feeling ever since I left Diana.

"Garth!" she fiercely whispered.

"Diana, what is it?"

"*He's* here!"

"Who is?"

"Si Buckles. He's in the backyard. Garth! I can hear him at the door! He's trying to get in!"

"I'm on my way."

Grabbing my keys, I ran to the garage where Jessie sat all snug and dry. I got in and turned the key. She crossfired and cut out. "Jessie, come on!" I tried again. She roared, sputtered, and died, as I pumped the accelerator in frustration. I tried once more. Unn . . . unn . . . unn . . . unn. I got out and slammed the door, cracking the glass. "Jessie, God damn you!"

I left the garage on the run, hurdled a hedge, and sprinted into the street. Part of me was saying this couldn't be happening, and the other part knew it was. Two blocks later everything began to blur, and all I could feel was the pain gouging my side. I ran harder, trying to beat the pain, which was slowly creeping through my chest into my throat. Stumbling up her walk, my legs two boards I couldn't feel, I crashed into Diana's front door.

"Garth! Is that you?" she asked from inside.

A thousand black crystals were dancing before me. Whoever called running a sport must've liked cockfights, too. "I think so."

She opened the door and helped me inside. "Are you all right?"

"Wait a minute." I walked across the kitchen and leaned

on the sink. I thought I was going to toss my cookies right there. But I didn't, and a few minutes later the room stopped spinning. A few minutes after that I could talk again. "I'm all right."

"Why didn't you drive?" She must've seen my ears light up and the smoke roll out of my nose. "Or should I ask?"

"You shouldn't ask." I tried my legs. They were working again. I walked to the window and looked outside. All I could see was the rain. "You're sure it was Si Buckles?"

"I'm sure."

"*Why* are you sure?"

"I don't know. But I'm sure."

"You saw his face then?"

"I saw him well enough to know it was Si Buckles."

"Where was he at the time?"

"Under the security light at the corner of the garage. I'd just taken a bath and was standing at the window watching the rain when I saw him. When he saw me, he started toward the house."

"What did *you* do?"

"What do you think I did? I screamed bloody murder. Then I called you."

"And after that?"

"He came to the back door. You remember I told you that. And, like a fool, I just stood there by the phone. Now, I can think of a hundred things I should have done, but I couldn't at the time."

"He tried to get in?"

"Yes. He tried the door several times. He almost broke it down."

"Did he say anything?"

"No. Nothing."

"Then he went away?"

"I guess. I haven't looked to find out."

"Why don't we now?"

We went to the back door and I examined it. She was right. He had worked it over. The strange thing was, it was unlocked. He hadn't tried to open it; he'd tried to go through it. Stepping outside, I scanned the yard. If he was still out here, he wasn't moving. That's about all I could tell for certain. I'd turned to come inside when I saw the roses lying in the yard. Diana saw them at the same time. She got there first.

"How did he know?" she asked, kneeling in the rain. "How did he know?"

"I don't understand."

She stood, handing me the roses. "It's my bouquet to Fran. It should be buried with him."

"Was your name on it?"

"No."

I looked at the roses. It was a beautiful pink bouquet, the buds still opening. "Do you want me to get rid of it?"

"No. Bring it inside. I'll take it back tomorrow."

"Are you sure you want to?"

She took them from me. "I'm sure."

We went inside where Diana cut the stems and put the roses in water. I looked at the clock. Midnight. I didn't believe it. It seemed much later. Walking into the bedroom, Diana returned with one of Fran's robes. It was then I realized I wasn't wearing a shirt or shoes. I put the robe on.

"Coffee?" she asked.

"No. I'm wound tight enough as it is."

"A drink then?"

"Scotch . . . on the rocks."

She poured us each one, then touched her glass to mine. "Good morning to you."

"May it go peacefully."

"Amen." She set her glass down. "He really *was* here, Garth. I didn't make it up."

"I know."

"What do you suppose he wanted?"

"I thought you could tell me."

"I hardly knew Si Buckles. There's nothing I have that he'd want."

"Maybe it's not Si Buckles."

"What's that supposed to mean?"

"He's on my mind and on your mind. He was on Phil's mind and Fran's mind. He might be a projection of our own thoughts."

"Garth, I *saw* him! I *heard* him at the door!"

"I'm not doubting you. But real phenomena can be mistaken for something else. What you see or hear is real, but not what you saw or heard. That's how swamp gas becomes a flying saucer."

"Then where did the roses come from?"

"I don't know."

"Why couldn't Si Buckles have brought them?"

"Diana, Si Buckles is *dead*!"

"All right, so he's dead. I don't believe in ghosts any more than you do, but I *do* believe my own eyes, and they saw Si Buckles tonight."

"It's too late to argue." I drained my glass of Scotch. "You have an extra blanket? I'm sleeping on the couch."

"Not in those wet clothes, you aren't. I'll get you some pajamas." She returned a few minutes later with a sheet, pillow, and blanket. "Your pajamas are in the bathroom. You can hang your clothes in the shower for now. I'll dry them in the morning."

I went to the bathroom, changed into Fran's pajamas, and returned to the couch, crawling under the blanket. "Smells good. Where's it been?"

"My cedar chest. It's the blanket we kids always took to the free show."

"I never took a blanket. I always sat in the grass with the chiggers."

"Why didn't you take a blanket?"

"Well, the free show was in the north end of town, and I lived in the east end of town. To get home, I always went across the airport. The airport was a long stretch of no

—— 133 ——

lights and high grass." I smiled at her. "You ever tried to outrun the Shadow carrying a blanket?"

She laughed. "You're serious, aren't you?"

"Ninety percent anyway."

"I can't ever imagine you being afraid of anything."

"There aren't many things I haven't been afraid of at one time or another." I closed my eyes. I was already drifting.

"Garth?"

"Yes?"

"Sweet dreams."

I didn't remember answering.

I awakened to the smell of bacon frying, lay for a moment remembering where I was, and sat up, as Diana came into the room. "You want pancakes or French toast?" she asked.

"Which is easier?"

I lay back down. Somewhere in the world is a comfortable couch, and someday perhaps I'll find it, but not yet. My back was in the shape of an S, and my legs felt like the Tooth Fairy had left me cement shoes along with the rock under my pillow. "I like your couch. Every masochist should have one."

"It was your choice, remember?" She raised me up, fluffed my pillow, and laid me back down. "Did you ever answer me?"

"French toast."

"Brown sugar or maple syrup?"

"Maple." I followed her into the kitchen and sat down heavily on one of the oak chairs. She brought me a cup of coffee, cream and sugar. "Do I look as bad as I feel?"

"You've looked better."

"Thanks. How's come you look so good?"

"I never went to bed."

"What were you doing?"

"Thinking mostly . . . about where I go from here."

"It'll come in time."

—— 134 ——

She smiled. "He says with the greatest of ease. By the way, your clothes are dry. You can borrow one of Fran's shirts to get home in."

After breakfast I walked home. It was a cool morning, the sun glaring white behind a thin veil of clouds, the trees wrapped in mist and sentry still. I enjoyed the walk. It shook out the cobwebs and stretched the cramps from my legs. Ruth was waiting for me at the door. She had the look of a mother who'd been up all night and didn't know whether to hug me or hit me.

"You could have called," she said, following me up the stairs.

"I didn't want to get you up."

"I was already up."

"I didn't know that."

"What were you doing?"

"You don't want to hear."

"Garth, he's not even cold yet!"

"It wasn't that. It was something else." I glanced at the pocket of her housecoat and saw a familiar sight. I picked it out of her pocket. "What's this?" I asked.

"Maybe nothing. But it kept me up most of the night thinking about it . . . while I was pacing the floor wondering what happened to you." She took the diary from me, marked a place, and handed it back. "Now, read it aloud."

I read it aloud. "'This will be the biggest one yet. The four of us will be waiting at Whyindot.'" I lowered the diary. "Whyindot? *Wyandotte!*" I smacked my hand against my leg. "That's it! Wyandotte! But see how he's spelled it. *Whyindot.* No wonder I missed it." I read on: "'Boy, he doesn't know what he's walking into. This is Fran's best plan, his baby. I wouldn't miss it for the world. Come on, tonight!'"

"Now read the next page," Ruth said.

I read the next page. "'Ho hum. What a boaring day. I think I'll go find Fran and see what he's up to. He wouldn't even speak to me in school. I think it's Dieanna. She never did like me. Sometimes I wish she was dead.'" I lowered the diary. "So? What's your point?"

"My point is, whatever happened to the big doings they had planned the night before?"

"Maybe it didn't come off. A lot of them never did."

"Read the date." I did. It was November 1, 1959. "Now read the date of the previous entry." I did. It was October 30, 1959. I still didn't see her point. "Thirty days has November, April, June, and September . . ." she said. "But I don't recall October being in the minority."

"There's a page missing!"

She smiled. "He might be slow, but there's still hope. The only question is, where did it go to?"

"You remember the night you heard somebody up here? *This* was the diary I'd been reading, but it wasn't the one I found on top. He could have taken it then."

"Why would he go to all of that trouble?"

"I don't know . . . unless there was something there he didn't want me to read."

"That was twenty-five years ago. What would it matter now?"

"That's what I'm going to try to find out."

The day was cool, as the morning had been, and the sky was mottled, like a hyena's coat, the sun barely bright enough to cast a shadow. It seemed less like spring than the day before, almost a step backwards into winter. After drying points, spark-plug wires, and distributor, I finally got Jessie started. I rode with the window up and the heater on.

Tillie wasn't home, but from her front porch I could see Ruben standing with his scythe beside Fran's grave. He wore his blotched leather jacket and a red baseball cap and reminded me of a statue I once saw on a city lawn. I went down to see him.

"Afternoon, Mr. Ryland." He didn't look at me.

"Afternoon, Ruben. You haven't seen Tillie, have you?"

He pointed. "I saw her go over the ridge this morning. I think she's hunting mushrooms."

"That's right. It is the season." He was staring at Fran's grave. "Something bothering you, Ruben?"

"He's awful young to be dead. It hardly seems right, does it? Life should be more fair than that."

"Someone once said, 'Where is it written that life should be fair?' I've always remembered that."

He shrugged and smiled as if he hadn't heard. "Diana Chesterson was here earlier. She left some roses for Fran."

"How long ago did she leave?"

"Long enough for me to get cold standing here."

I blew into my hands to warm them. "That wouldn't be too long." Ruben was looking away. He was more distant today than usual. "What's wrong, Ruben?"

He continued to stare. "Nothing's wrong, Mr. Ryland."

"Is it Fran?"

"No. It's someone else, someone I knew a long time ago."

"Diana?"

The peelings from his leather jacket quivered in the wind. "She *is* a beautiful woman, isn't she, Mr. Ryland? But, no, I'm thinking about someone else."

"Si Buckles?"

His smile retreated to the corners of his mouth. "We were friends once, did you know that? There was nothing we wouldn't do for each other. But something happened . . . I don't know what . . . Maybe it was because I was at the top of our class and he was near the bottom, but he started hating me. He still does, Mr. Ryland—to this day."

"Si Buckles is dead," I reminded him.

His full smile returned. "Oh, I know, Mr. Ryland, but sometimes I can still see him in my sleep, and he's shaking his fist at me and saying, 'You're next, Ruben. You're next.' What do you suppose he means by that?"

"I wouldn't worry about it, Ruben," I said, though now I

was worried. "You know how dreams are. They're not as real as we make them out to be."

"I'm not worried, Mr. Ryland. There's nothing more that Si Buckles can do to me now."

"What did he do to you, Ruben? Do you remember?" But he didn't answer.

"Damn!" Tillie yelled, as she came over the ridge toward us. "There ought to be a law against greenbriers!" She carried a sack and a walking stick and nodded as she approached us. "Howdy, Ruben, Garth. Kind of cold to be jawing, isn't it?"

I turned up the collar on my jacket. "Now that you mention it. Ruben, I'll see you later."

He was still aloof. "Sure, Mr. Ryland."

Tillie and I started across the cemetery toward her house. "What's with him today?" Tillie asked.

"I don't know."

"Mr. Ryland?" Ruben had turned to face us.

"Yes, Ruben?"

"Nothing. I wanted to say good-bye." He turned and picked up a flower from Fran's grave before disappearing into the woods.

"That's what he reminds me of," Tillie said, staring after him, "a cut flower. No matter how hard you try, he'll never bloom again." She studied me. "You walking for the exercise or because you like my company?"

"Both."

"I know you're lying, but keep it up."

We continued on. "I've got a question only you can answer," I said.

"If you want my middle name, forget it. I have. Anything else I might speculate on."

"Do you know where Ruben went the night he lost his mind?"

"I might."

"Just nod if I'm right. Wyandotte?"

— 138 —

She nodded. "Yep. That's it. He told me that afternoon he was going there that night."

"Did he say why?"

"Nope. You know how kids are. They're always sniffing somewhere they don't belong. Ruben was no exception."

"Thanks, Tillie. I think I know why."

"It's a shame, too. He was a real bright boy. Have him show you his awards sometime." We stopped at the bottom of her hill where Jessie was parked. "Well, here's where I get off. You never did ask what was in my sack."

"I can guess."

"Do you want some?"

"If you have some to spare."

She emptied part of the morels into her apron and gave the sack to me. "They're mostly grey and black sponge. The yellows haven't come on yet. I doubt they will, now that it's turned off cool."

She trudged up the hill, while I drove back to town. Parking a block away from Diana's, I sat in the car holding the diary. One line had stuck like a cocklebur in my throat. "The *four* of us will be waiting at Whyindot." Si Buckles, Phil Chesterson, Fran Baldwin, and. . . ? I glanced at the sun. It looked like the yolk of a poached egg. It was that kind of day.

Diana was in the kitchen and came running when she saw me at the door. I looked down at the diary and back up at her. She studied me a moment, then led me inside. "Okay, what have I done?" she asked.

"You didn't tell me what happened at Wyandotte."

"I see." I unzipped my jacket and she helped me slide out of it. "Well, don't stand there like a storm trooper. Come in and sit down." I followed her into the family room, as she dropped my jacket in Fran's chair. We sat together on the couch. "What do you want to know about Wyandotte?"

"Were you there?"

"Yes, I was there."

"Did you know what they had planned for Ruben?"

"No. Not until it was too late."

"Were you the reason Ruben was there?"

She stared at me. "Come again?"

"How did Fran and the others get him there?"

"I don't know. They never said." I saw the question in her eyes. "Do you?"

"Remember the beech I told you about, the one with your initials carved on it? Ruben didn't do that for exercise. He did it because he was in love with you."

"Garth, I was only fourteen years old! I wasn't interested in Ruben or anyone else! I was just Phil's tag-along kid sister."

"You were the bait! How else would they get Ruben out there?"

"If I was, *I* didn't know it!"

"Then why did you go along?"

She rose and walked to the fireplace where she slowly traced the veins of mortar. "All right. I went because Fran asked me to. He had before . . . several times, but I always said no. This time I said yes. It's as simple as that."

"Did the others know you were going?"

"I don't know. Probably not. They wouldn't have approved of taking a girl along."

"But they *could* have?"

"Yes, they could have." Her hand had stopped and now rested on the mantle. "It seemed so innocent . . . so absurd really. We were kids, all of us. We didn't intend to hurt anyone."

"Do you know what they did to Ruben?"

"Not exactly. They told me to wait in the car. They didn't say why. They just told me to wait in the car. A short while later I saw Ruben cross the clearing and go into the house. As soon as he was inside, they barred the doors and went into their act. I begged them to let him out, but they wouldn't listen to me. Finally, I pushed Phil aside and went inside myself. It was too late. His mind was already gone . . . And in his hand . . ." She was looking at her own hand, "was a note in my handwriting asking him to meet me there in Hull House by the stairway. Except I never wrote it. One of the girls in Fran's class had."

"Who was inside with Ruben?"

"Fran was inside. Phil and Si are the ones who guarded the doors." She leaned against the fireplace, closing her eyes. "Fran never got over it. It was as though his life and Ruben's were both lost that night. He seemed the same. It wasn't until years later when he almost had a mental breakdown that I learned how deeply it had affected him." She opened her eyes to look at me. "Fran was an enigma—to himself, to his friends, and to me. He was so handsome and so gifted and so easy to love that I don't think he ever questioned the source of his strength—his soul, if you will. Remember the line of Frost's: 'God, if You'll forgive my little jokes on Thee, I'll forgive Thy great big one on me.' I believe that's the way Fran felt about his life, that because everything came so easily to him, he was never the man he should have been. And when a real crisis came, as it did with Ruben, he wasn't equal to it." Her eyes never retreated, and I felt their heat in my skull. "But I'm not guilty, Garth. The only reason I didn't tell you before was because it's past, and I believe in letting the past stay buried."

"I had to ask—for my own peace of mind."

"You've asked, and I've answered. Now where do we go from here?"

"Si Buckles, was he blackmailing Fran?"

"No. At least there was no money involved."

"How do you know?"

"I kept our books."

"Then why did Fran hate Si and why did Si hate you?"

"Fran's jokes were a sickness. I tried to get him to stop, and he did for a while, the years we were away in residency and medical school. But shortly after we moved back here, Si came over one night, and it started all over again. I told

Fran we should move away and put it all behind us, but he could never take that step." She glanced around the room at her antiques. "And the longer it went on, the less I tried. I had my painting and my home and all the security I ever wanted. It wasn't a bad life . . ." She saw me staring out the window. "What are you thinking, that I sold myself too cheaply?"

"I'm trying to think of why Si hated you."

"I wasn't aware that he did."

"He said as much in his diaries."

"Frankly, Garth, I don't think he was capable of it. He seemed a gentle soul really, more lost than anything else. But he was poison for Fran. He clung to him like a leech. And yes, Fran really did hate him."

"Enough for Fran to kill him?"

"No. Fran would never do that. He valued life too highly. But enough to stop just short of it."

I walked to the phone and dialed Rupert. No one answered.

"Whom were you calling?" Diana asked.

"Sheriff Roberts. I want him to assign a man to you."

"Garth, I won't have it! I'm not a house plant you need to feed and water!"

"You won't even know he's there."

"Why are you doing this?"

"Because I love you, and if anything happened to you, I'd never forgive myself. If that's not enough reason, you can kick me out right now because I plan to live here until this is over."

"That's your final word?"

"That's my final word."

Her smile could turn me inside out, and she knew it. "Then go get your things, while I put supper on."

CHAPTER 11

It frosted in the night, a light frost that glazed the lawns and melted quickly in the sun. I sat in my office with my newspaper column in front of me. It wasn't the story I wanted to write, but it would have to do. I got up, walked to the window, and killed the fly that had been buzzing me for the last hour. I felt better. If a dead fly in May kept thousands away, a dead fly in April should be worth a million.

The printer came in, and I gave him my column to read. He sat down, rubbed his chin twice, and yawned. A few minutes later, he handed it back to me.

"Better than last week," he said.

"That's all?"

"Oh, it's good enough. But I was expecting more. You know on T.V. how the music gets all wrought up right before the murder. Well, this is the music without the murder."

"Wait a minute." I took it from him and put it into my typewriter. I typed five words and gave it back to him.

He read the five words I'd written: Next week—the Last Laugh. "For sure?"

"I hope."

"You're going out on a limb, aren't you?"

"Way out."

"I admire your guts, for what it's worth. Why are you doing it?"

"Added incentive. I work better under a deadline."

The phone rang. "Garth?"

"Yes, Rupert?"

"Can you spare a minute?"

"What's on your mind?"

"Looks like another break-in at the hardware."

"I'll be there."

Fifteen minutes later I met him in front of the hardware. His hands were stuffed in his jacket pockets, and his sallow face was almost ruddy. He spit in disgust on the sidewalk. "Where in the hell did spring go?" he asked. "I'm going to have to haul out my woolies again."

"It'll be back."

"Yeah, about August. How goes your investigation?"

"It goes."

"I sympathize with you. Lord knows how many dead ends I've come to in my day. Just keep plodding, that's my only advice. It doesn't earn you any medals, but maybe some satisfaction along the way." He found a patch of sunlight and stepped into it. "At least, it's been quiet the last couple days—until now."

I studied the hardware door. "It looks like the same window's broken."

"Yep. The exact same one."

"Anything taken?"

"Not that I know of. You're welcome to look."

We went inside and I surveyed the store, while Rupert stood over a register. Nothing seemed out of place. "Do you think something scared them off before they got inside?" I asked.

He held his hands to the register. "It seems like it. They were probably kids from what I can tell."

"Why do you say that?"

"Kids break windows to get inside. Pros have better, quieter ways. Besides, no pro would break into a hardware

—— 144 ——

unless he had a semi to haul the goods away. There's no percentage otherwise."

"I wonder why they came back?"

"Maybe on a dare. I got my share of watermelons that way. My share of rock salt, too. That's what finally broke me of it." He rubbed his rump. "That and my daddy's razor strap." He still stood on the register. "Unless you think Si Buckles has been here? But in his present form I don't think he'd need to break a window to get in."

"I'm not sure what his present form is."

"Would you like to explain that?"

"If I could. Rupert, I have a favor."

"Name it."

"I need someone to watch Diana Baldwin for me."

"You're sure she's in danger?"

"As I can be under the circumstances."

"I can't spare a man right now. Maybe in a couple days. But I can double the patrol past there."

"Anything would help."

He was thinking, his bloodhound eyes slowly rolling from side to side. "What are the circumstances that you're under?"

"Si Buckles. He's been at Diana's door. He's even tried to break it down. Perhaps with good reason." He didn't move, not even a twitch of his eyebrows. "Rupert?"

"I'm here. I'm just waiting for that shiver to get done crawling up my spine."

I saw something on the floor and knelt to pick it up. I handed it to him. "What does this look like to you?"

"Blue clay." He felt it. "*Wet* blue clay. You have any on your shoes?"

"Not that I know of." I checked to make sure.

"Me either. It must've been somebody else."

"Has anyone else been in here besides us this morning?"

"Fritz. But he wouldn't track up his own store."

"You have to go down quite a ways for blue clay, don't you?" I asked.

"Yeah, about four feet most places around here."

"Then how would anyone get it on his shoes?"

"I was going to ask you the same thing." He thought a moment. "Of course, it'd be easy if you were walking around a construction site, or a dam, or a . . ." He was trying to swallow.

"Grave?"

"You said it, not me. Si Buckles *did* work here, didn't he?"

"Every day of his working life . . . except Sundays."

He took off his badge and laid it on the counter. "Well, that's it, folks, I'm off to Florida. I tell you, Garth, I've had it. If it ain't Si Buckles, it's Tillie. I think her goat's in love with my sheepskin jacket. Just yesterday he ate part of the sleeve." He tossed me the lump of blue clay. "Go make a pot or something with it, will you?"

I handed back his badge. "You'll feel better after coffee."

He pinned it back on. "Fat chance."

I walked to the mortuary and climbed the back stairs to Si Buckles' old bedroom. One look told me what I needed to know. The floor *was* tracked with clumps of blue clay. So what did it prove? That whoever was in the hardware had also been here? Maybe. But why? What was he doing here? What could he learn in this dim, musty room that not even a monk could love? I kicked a piece of clay into the register and heard it rattle all the way down to the basement. I felt my heart thud all the way down to my toes. The last laugh!

I walked home, as feathery clouds dulled the sun, and a cold, east wind bit into my face. Climbing the stairs to my study, I found Si Buckles' last diary and the entry I was looking for: "Doc has just told me I have a year at most to live. It's a rare disease, and always fatal. It starts in the bone marrow and spreads throughout the body. That's why I've been so weak lately. Doc says the medicine will only help for a while. I don't mind. I've had my share of fun. I'd just like to have one last laugh sometime before I die. Doc and Phil keep promising me, but they've never told me what they're planning. I sure hope they don't wait too long!!"

"Ruth, come here!"

She appeared a moment later. "Yes, Bwana?"

"Did Si Buckles look like he was dying to you?"

"What kind of question's that? I'm not a doctor."

"Give me your best laywoman's opinion."

"No, I thought the little turnip would live to haunt me forever." She caught herself. "Do you mind if I rephrase that?"

"He didn't look like he was dying to me either. What if he didn't die, what if he were murdered, who'd have the last laugh then?"

"Do you want to run that by me again? I'm not sure I heard you right."

"I was just thinking out loud."

"Well, I'd just as soon you'd keep those thoughts to yourself. We keep saying *he*, Garth. What if he isn't a he, but . . ." Her eyes had a fixed, glassy stare, like those of a puppet. ". . . something else? Shouldn't we leave well enough alone?"

"I don't know, Ruth. Maybe we should. Maybe there *are* mysteries in this life that are better left alone. But who was Si Buckles really? A harmless fool who lived and died for nothing? That's all he was a few weeks ago . . . until I got my hands on his diaries. That's the frightening thing. Sometimes I think he's my creation, that, as Dr. Frankenstein, I've turned a monster loose on the world. Except mine is a monster of the mind." I thumbed through the pages of Si's last diary. "There's another thing that bothers me. You say he helped put saltpeter in the town's water supply. Why isn't that in here? Or the trick he pulled on Robbie Davis? Or several others that have been brought to my attention? You've read these diaries as much as I have. Don't *you* ever wonder about them?"

"In what way?"

"Well, people who write diaries must like to write, or

they wouldn't go to the trouble. And they're probably sober, reflective people who like to read as well. As far as I can tell about Si, about the only thing he read was a thermometer. You see what I'm driving at? Si wasn't literate in any sense of the word. His keeping a diary is as unlikely as my keeping a horse in the backyard."

She gave it some serious thought. I could tell she'd had some doubts of her own. "But if Si didn't write these diaries, then who did?" she asked.

"That's what I'd like to know."

I drove out Fair Haven Road toward Broken Claw. It was quiet for spring—no tractors humming, no robins singing, no children out and about, puncturing the stillness with their springtime laughter. I glanced to my right where the smoke from someone's chimney hung limp, like the bent wick of a candle, never rising above the tree line, while the sun now shone through grey slats of clouds that began to slowly close like a venetian blind. I rolled up the window and closed the outside vent to save what heat I could.

Beside me on the seat was Si Buckles' last diary. I had two choices. I could throw it into Hog Run as I had the grocery-sack note, or I could try to find the note and compare the two. It would be easy to throw the diary into Hog Run—for somebody else maybe, not me. I *had* to know the truth. Then I'd decide what to do with it.

I parked Jessie along the road and climbed down the steep embankment beneath Broken Claw. Below, Hog Run slipped along without a sound, its somber surface a perfect mirror of the day. Above, a hemlock stood at attention, not even a ripple in its dark green foliage. It made me uneasy, too aware of myself.

I walked east. Downstream. It was dim here in the gorge and getting dimmer by the minute. I stopped to rest and wipe some sweat from my eye. I heard a stone trickling down the wall of the ravine toward me. It bounced once at my feet and then into Hog Run, making a soft *plurp!* as it did. I looked up, expecting to see a fox squirrel scurrying for the nearest tree. Instead I saw the figure of a man. Or what I thought was a man. Though I never took my eyes off of him, he began to melt into the hemlocks, until it seemed I was staring more at shadow than substance. Si Buckles? No, that wasn't possible. But something about him, the way an unexpected shaft of sunlight caught and held him for a moment, warned me it was. I told myself to get going, that there was no future in staying here.

There was one chance in a million I'd find the grocery-sack note. But I did. It had fallen into Hog Run and drifted downstream until it caught in a thornbush where it nestled high and dry as the waters of Hog Run receded. Then I wouldn't have found it if I hadn't looked down at the exact right moment. All of which made me wonder. About me. About God. About the chain of events we often call coincidence. Some things were meant to be. I knew that much. But I didn't know enough to say why.

"Si Buckles lives." The message was still the same, though somewhat blurred by the elements. I compared the writing in the note to that in Si's last diary. The light was bad, and I was no expert, but the writing looked the same. Since I received the message the night Si was buried, it meant one of two things. Someone other than Si wrote it and the diaries. Or Si Buckles did indeed live!

I drove back to town as the first drops of rain hit Jessie's windshield. Diana's kitchen light was on, and from the outside looking in, it was the warmest, brightest light I knew. I knocked and she came to the door wearing a beige pants suit and a ruffled blue apron. "I ought to leave you out in the rain," she said. "I will the next time you knock."

"Habit."

"Well, break it." She took my coat into the bedroom. "How about a fire?" I asked.

"Fine with me."

I soon had a fire built, and I sat close to it, close enough to feel its heat draw the chill from me. Diana brought me a brandy, along with one for herself, and together we sat watching the fire. "Supper's ready," she said. "We can eat whenever you want."

"In a few minutes."

"You seem preoccupied. Is something wrong?"

"Yes, but I don't know yet how wrong. Where did Fran keep his medical records?"

"At the clinic."

"Are they still there?"

"I think so. Why?"

"I'd like to look at them tomorrow morning."

"Any particular reason?"

"It'll become clearer as we go along. What hospital did Phil usually go to when someone had a heart attack?"

"Lately he went to St. Mary's at Hay Rapids. They have a new cardiac unit there."

"Do you mind if I use your phone?"

"Go ahead. I just remembered I have to make gravy."

I found the number and dialed St. Mary's. "The admittance desk, please."

"This is Mrs. Swalley, may I help you?"

"Yes. This is Garth Ryland from the *Oakalla Reporter*, and a friend of mine was admitted to your hospital at the end of March, but I'm uncertain of the date. I wouldn't ask, but we're running a special feature on him."

"What's your friend's name?"

"Si Buckles."

"Let me check." I waited while she checked. "I'm sorry, Mr. Ryland, but we have no record for Si Buckles."

"I believe he was dead on arrival."

"Well, it's very possible then that he was never admitted."

"Then could you switch me to emergency?"

"Certainly. Hold on."

"Mrs. Bailey here."

"Garth Ryland here. I'm looking for the nurse on duty early the morning of March 29th."

There was a pause. I thought perhaps she'd fallen asleep. "How early?" she finally asked.

"Three or four A.M."

Another pause. She wasn't going to leap without looking. "That'd be me."

"You knew Dr. Baldwin, didn't you?"

"I might have. Why?"

"Did he have a D.O.A. that morning?"

"Who wants to know?"

"An old friend. And his wife, among others. It's important."

She thought it over and decided in my favor. "No."

"You're sure?"

"Absolutely."

"Thank you very much."

She didn't answer. I felt lucky to learn what I had.

I called the county hospital to make sure. The answer was the same. Si Buckles was never there.

"The gravy's ready. Are you ready to eat it?" Diana asked from the kitchen.

"I'm on my way." I sat at the table while she carried a roast from the oven. "How did your day go?" I asked.

"It's funny you should ask that." She set the roast on the table and walked to the wastebasket, withdrawing a bouquet of withered roses. "I found these outside the back door after you left this morning."

"Are they the same ones again?"

She dropped them back into the wastebasket. "Yes." I held her chair as she sat across from me. "That's not all. I drove out to Wyandotte today to see the beech you told me about, you know, the one with my initials on it. They're there all right—with a very large X carved through them."

"Ruben's initials, too?"

"Yes."

"The X wasn't there when I saw them."

"I didn't think it was." She passed me the browned potatoes. "Eat your supper before it gets cold."

"There were *five*, not four of you at Wyandotte. Counting Ruben."

"What do you mean by that?"

"I'm not sure exactly."

"Do you think he's in some kind of danger?"

"He might be."

"From whom?"

"Whoever's after you."

"No one's after me for certain. The whole thing could be a joke—a bad joke."

"That's what it might seem like to you, but not to me."

"I'm not going to crack, Garth. You won't find me with a bullet in my brain. So stop worrying."

"Do you mind if I take it a step further?"

"Not if you'll eat your supper." She passed me a basket of sourdough biscuits.

I took one and buttered it. "You have jelly?"

"Strawberry preserves."

"That'll do." She got them for me. "The question is, why did Fran and Phil kill themselves? Now, there's no obvious answer, and the less than obvious answer, that they saw Si Buckles' ghost, leaves too much unexplained. Even if they did, it's hardly worth killing yourself over—unless, of course, they killed Si."

"Garth!"

"Let me finish. Now, there's another possibility. Say they planned to kill Si and he found out about it and somehow escaped. So what they saw wasn't Si's ghost at all, but Si himself. If that's the case, Si might have every reason in the world to come after you next."

"I don't like either explanation."

"I have another. Would you like to hear it?"

"No. Let's talk about something else."

"Okay. What did you do the rest of the day?"

"I went job hunting."

"Where?"

"Madison."

"Any luck?"

"I got two offers and two maybes. They said I could name my own hours."

"That sounds fair enough."

"Maybe I should explain. One of the offers definitely wasn't for my sketches. The other was, but suggested we talk further—at his place over dinner."

"Are you going?"

"Do you think I'd tell you if I was?"

"And the maybes?"

"With one I can work part time and get paid just enough for mileage. With the other I get to carry coffee and to water the plants. No one seemed to care that I had a degree in graphic arts."

"Why don't you work for me?"

"Doing what?"

"Illustrations—maybe a cartoon. I know some people in the business. Maybe we can syndicate you."

"How much will it pay?"

"That depends on how good you are."

"I have a folder full of sketches I can show you."

"I'll look at them after supper."

"You're really serious? It's not a handout?"

"No. I've liked everything of yours I've seen. In fact, I'd like to see your portrait of Ruben again."

"Right now?"

"If you don't mind." She brought it to me and I studied it as I ate. "This *is* your best, no question about it."

"I'm glad you approve."

"Has Ruben seen it?"

"No, I think you're the only one I've shown it to. You understand why, don't you? No one else would understand."

I studied his eyes and smile. "It's not so much understanding as it is believing. You saw it first, didn't you?"

"What's that?"

"His sanity."

"Ruben makes a lot of sense sometimes."

"Yes, he does, a lot of sense."

"So who's to say what's the real world, ours or Ruben's?"

"Why don't you ask him?"

"I might do that."

By the time we finished supper and the dishes, the fire had burned down to a few white coals that barely sparked when I stoked them. I added more wood and watched the fire quickly take hold again. Diana sat behind me, pulling me against her. I knew by the way she held me, and the way I felt, I wasn't going anywhere else tonight.

"You're very soft, you know that?" I said.

"Don't talk."

We sat silent for a long time, as the fire blazed up, blackening the logs, then gradually fell, leaving one grey-red hourglass that seemed to melt into the grate below. It was still raining. I could hear it peck the windows, while the fire held back the gloom like a small, red dome.

I lay with my head in Diana's lap, and she lay very still, nearly asleep. I rose, and she moved weakly to stop me, but I said, "I'm just getting more wood." I returned with the wood, then covered her with the afghan.

Her eyes were softly glazed. "I'm sorry."

"For what?"

"Fading out on you."

"I'm glad you can. You need the sleep."

She smiled. "When I was little, I used to imagine I had this invincible shield to protect me from the world. Nothing could get through it if I didn't want it to. Sometimes with you I feel like that little girl again." Her eyes closed and she was asleep.

It rained all night and was raining the next morning—not as hard, but I could see it streak the windows as I put the coffee on. Diana still slept before the fire. I'd slept some, mostly in snatches, and the rest of the time I tended the fire.

I went into the bathroom, found Fran's razor, and began to shave. Diana came in, kissed me, and left her housecoat on my arm as she stepped into the shower. I laid her housecoat on the clothes hamper. "What do you want for breakfast?" I asked.

"Do you have a specialty?"

"Cereal and juice."

"That'll be fine."

"How about oatmeal with raisins?"

"How about oatmeal with raisins and *honey*?"

"That I can handle." The mirror was steaming up. "You realize you're making it hard to shave."

"Sorry. I'll be through in a minute."

"Leave the water on." I began to undress.

"Will do." She stepped out of the shower a moment later. I held her towel. "Could you get my back, please?" I did. She turned to face me. "Now, the rest of me."

"Why don't I turn off the shower first?"

"Why don't you?"

I scorched the oatmeal, but neither of us minded. The

coffee was good anyway. She smiled lazily at me, then leaned back in the chair and closed her eyes. "Why don't we stay home and bake bread today?" she asked.

"I'd like nothing better."

"But . . ." Her eyes opened. "I heard a *but* in there."

"We have other things to do."

She got up and poured more coffee. "Do I have to get dressed first?"

"I'd advise it."

A half hour later we drove to Fran's clinic. The rain continued to fall, and the clouds were now in black humps with white, swirling tops like the waves of an angry sea. Unlocking the door and turning on the lights, Diana led me into Fran's office. As I stepped onto the burgandy carpet and saw the walnut paneling, I was struck by its beauty. My offices came in one color—institutional green. "Do you know where he kept his records?" I asked.

"The active file is in the top drawer of his cabinet, the inactive file in the drawer below it. The key is in the top right-hand drawer of his desk. If you don't mind, I'm going out into the waiting room for a while."

"I'll see you out there."

I looked through the inactive file first, but there was no record of Si Buckles. I checked the active file. It was in there. I read through it, then more slowly the second time. I found what I wanted to know.

In the waiting room Diana was standing at the window watching the rain. Her grey-blue eyes were trancelike, seeming to touch infinity with their perception. Sometimes I wondered how much of her I really knew. "What did you find?" she asked.

"Do you want to sit down?"

"No. I'd rather watch the rain."

"Do you mind if I sit down?"

"Be my guest."

I sat down and scanned the file before me. "I found Si's record in the active file. Is that unusual?"

"No. Fran was never very well organized, and his office help were hired for . . . let's say *other* reasons than their clerical efficiency."

"Then it's not unusual that I found no record of Si's death?"

"A little, but understandable under the circumstances."

"Or no record of Si's heart attack?"

"They came at the same time."

"Or no record of Si's bone marrow disease?"

She turned from the window, crossed the room and sat beside me. "That *is* unusual. Are you sure it's not there? Fran's handwriting was notoriously bad."

I handed her the file. "Take a look."

She handed it back a moment later. "You're right."

"There's another thing I'm curious about. Remember in Si's diary he mentioned how weak he was, how that was a symptom of his disease. Could he have been anemic?"

"There's one way to find out. If Fran wrote a prescription, we can look for it in Si's medicine cabinet."

I put the file back and we drove to Si Buckles' house in Diana's Bentley. Jessie was still parked on the street. I had too many places to go today to depend on her.

Leaving Diana in the car, I ran inside, but couldn't beat the rain. I was soaked through, even my shadow was wet. I went into the bathroom and opened the medicine cabinet. It was jammed full of patent medicine for everything from plantar warts to jock itch. Five minutes later I had two dark prescription bottles dated at approximately the same time Si wrote of his disease.

I'd started from the bathroom when I saw the lump of blue clay lying in the hall. Another one lay a few feet beyond it. Both crumpled to powder when I squeezed them. They'd been there for some time. Entering Si's bedroom, I glanced into his open closet at the green shirts hanging inside. I felt myself recoil. For a moment I thought it was Si himself standing there.

Climbing into the car, I handed the prescription bottles to Diana. "Can you decipher these?"

"No, but I'll hold them for you."

The rain fell with a vengeance now, flooding the streets and washing gullies in the newly seeded lawns. I parked the Bentley in front of the drugstore and ran inside where the pharmacist sat reading a magazine. I handed him the bottles. "Spencer, could you tell me what's in these without breaking any rules?"

He read the labels. "Probably not, but I'll tell you anyway. The one on the left is methapyrilene, a sedative, and the one on the right is mostly ferrous sulfate—iron, in other words."

"Was Si anemic?"

"It looks like it."

"Was there anything else wrong with him?"

"Nothing physical. Of course, he always was a little jumpy. That's what the sedative's for. I could usually tell the minute he walked in here when he was up to something. He would swell up like a balloon about to burst."

"Do you remember the last time that was?"

He thought a moment. "A Thursday. The same day he died."

"Off the record, Spencer, do you think it's possible to scare a man to death?"

"That depends on the man."

"Si Buckles?"

"Very possible."

"Thanks, Spencer, you've been a big help."

"Anytime." He returned to his magazine.

"Well?" Diana asked when I returned to the Bentley.

"He was anemic."

"That's all?"

"As far as I know."

"Where to now?"

"Si Buckles' nearest living relative."

I drove home. Ruth was in the living room watching her favorite soap opera. "Lunch is on the stove. I'll be with you in a minute," she said.

"I can't stay," I answered. "I need the list of all those who attended Si's funeral."

"It's in the buffet, top, middle drawer . . ." She caught up with the conversation. "You want *what?*"

I studied her and smiled. "I'm getting warm, aren't I?"

"I don't know what you're talking about."

"To what you saw?"

"I didn't see anything. I felt it . . ." She stared at her hand outstretched in front of her, then watched it close into a fist. "That's all I'm going to say."

"Did you get it?" Diana asked, as I slid in beside her. "Reluctantly."

She flipped through it. "It's a long list. We could spend a week on it and still not learn anything."

"I've thought of that. You were there before I was. Who do you remember viewing the body?"

"Why don't you read through the list? It might jog my memory."

I began reading. She stopped me on the fifteenth name. I lowered the list and sighed. "Bertha Thompkins. You're sure?"

"Yes. She took one of Si's flowers, plucked all the petals off of it, and blew them in his face."

"That's very touching."

"You have to call them as you see them."

Bertha Thompkins was home. She showed me inside, as her tomcat sauntered up and raked his claws down my pants leg. When Bertha turned to sit down, I kicked the tom halfway across the room, but he came right back. "Freddie likes you," she observed. "He wants to play."

Freddie was finding the skin under my pants. I reached down and pushed him away. Ears laid back, he pounced for my hand and caught a foot instead. "Freddie plays a little rough."

She sighed. "I know. I think the neighborhood children tease him. Freddie! Here, Kitty! Be a nice boy!" Freddie had ten claws and all of his teeth sunk into my shoe. He wasn't about to leave.

"Freddie," I bent down, grabbing him by the nape, as he yowled in protest, "why don't you go outside and play?" I carried him to the door and dropped him on the porch.

"Freddie hates the rain," was all she said. Then she got up and began to water her plants. Ten minutes later she was still watering, and I had the message. I stepped outside, as Freddie shot past me on his way back in.

"What did you find out?" Diana asked on my return.

"Freddie hates the rain."

"I see. Was she a subscriber?"

"I'd like to hope not."

"Old people are funny about their pets. That's all some of them have."

I rubbed my leg. "With good reason."

"Why don't you let me try?"

"It's a waste of time."

"Give me five minutes?"

"You have it."

I rested my head on the seat and listened to the rain lightly drum the windshield. The trees were still, the sky a Confederate grey, and the rain fell straight down, barely rippling the new, yellow leaves. It was comfortable there, fragrant with the lingering scent of Diana's perfume. I closed my eyes and waited.

The door swung open and Diana climbed in beside me. "You're right. It was a waste of time."

"Nothing?"

"I can't say that." She raised her pants leg to show me the claw marks. "She did talk to me, though. She wanted to know who did my hair."

"Who does?"

"I do it myself."

"Does she want you to do hers?"

"No. She doesn't like it." She glanced back at the house. "The old witch."

We started down the list again. Eight names later she stopped me. I shook my head in disbelief. "Edgar Shoemaker. You're batting a thousand."

"Why don't *I* read the list and *you* try to remember?"

"Forget I said anything."

We drove to Edgar Shoemaker's welding shop, and I got out, jumped a mud puddle, and squeezed through his half-opened door. It was dark and damp inside, and I had to ease my way around the junk on the floor. Edgar was sitting at his welding table, smoking a cigar. He'd lost an eye, a lung, and he wheezed when he talked.

"Afternoon, Edgar."

He squinted at me through the smoke. "Is that you, Garth? Come closer so I can see you." I came closer, close enough to feel the heat from the welder. "What brings *you* in here?"

"I'd like to ask you a couple questions."

"Wait a minute." He laid down his cigar and pulled down his welding mask. "Step back, will you? I want to give this one more shot." He did, as I turned away and shaded my eyes. Turning off the welder, he plunged the piece of steel he was welding into a tank of water. The hot steel hissed, as a small cloud of steam rose up from the tank.

"What *is* that anyway?" I asked.

"The shaft to my lawn mower. I hit a rock."

"That's what I thought it was."

"It'll be good as new when I'm done with it." He set the shaft down and wiped his hands on his coveralls. "You said you had some questions?"

"Yeah. How well did you know Si Buckles?"

"Not near as good then as I do now. I'd kind of like to take my flowers back."

"Did you get a good look at Si when Phil showed him?"

"Garth, I ain't had a good look at nothing for the last ten

years. I got steel in one eye and God knows what in the other. I'm lucky to find my ass with both hands."

"But you did see him in the casket?"

"I saw him. I think it was him. It was supposed to be anyway."

"You played poker with him, didn't you?"

"Yep. Every Thursday."

"How was he the Thursday he died?"

"Fine. Right up until he had his heart attack. Seemed fit as a fiddle as the saying goes."

"No chest pains while he was playing?"

"Not so I could notice. Though he *was* pretty well wound up, even for Si. Talked a mile a minute through the whole game. Then just as we were getting ready to leave, he grabbed his chest and keeled over. Dead, it looked like to me. Though Ben Pullam swore Si still had a good steady pulse when Doc Baldwin got there."

"What time was that?"

"Sometime after midnight. Doc took one look, and the next thing I knew he and Phil Chesterson were carting Si off in the hearse. Or ambulance as the case may be. It doubled for both when Phil was alive."

"Thanks, Edgar."

"And thanks to you for dropping by. It sometimes gets lonesome up at this end of town."

"Down at my end, too."

He struck an arc and relighted his cigar. "Aw, what the hell! We'll get by all right."

Diana stared at me as I got inside the car. "Don't say it," I said. "I know I need a shower."

"How could you get so dirty between here and there?"

"I've never been able to figure it out. I could see my clothes darken just standing there."

"Any luck?"

"Some."

"I've got another customer for you."

"Who's that?"

"Cecil Edwards. We'd better hurry, though. He closes at five."

I walked into Cecil Edwards' jewelry shop at one minute to five. At five he pulled the shade and locked the door. "Have to," he said, "or they'll be stringing in here until I've got a cold supper. Now, what can I do for you, Garth? I've bought about all the space I can afford."

"You've been reading my column?"

"I never miss it. It's the first thing I do when I get the mail."

"You know then I'm doing a feature on Si Buckles. Seeing him for the last time, would you say he'd changed much over the years?"

"Not a whit. He looked the same at forty as he did at twenty. Maybe a little heavier, that's all."

"I only knew him for five years. I wasn't sure."

"And Phil did a good job, too. I never saw anyone so lifelike. Even his color was good." He seemed eager to talk about it to someone.

"That's funny, Cecil. I was getting ready to ask you that."

He walked to the east window, peered outside, then pulled the shade. Crossing the room, he pulled the shade on the west window. "But you know the strangest thing . . ." His voice fell to a whisper, as he glanced quickly around the room. "It's eerie even to talk about it." He wiped his eyes with his handkerchief. "The strangest thing was seeing that watch of his still *running*."

"He was wearing a watch?"

"*Yes*! It seems I've worked on it a hundred times. I told him to break down and buy a new one, but he never did. He just kept putting new parts in the old one." He walked to the door and peeped under the shade. Satisfied, he returned to me. "But it's not the watch itself that bothered me so much." He shrugged, "They might as well bury him with it on. Nobody else would want it." He leaned across the counter toward me. "No. It wasn't the watch. It was the fact that it was *running*. What's the sense of winding the watch of a dead man? He's not going anywhere."

"You might have a point, Cecil."

"I wouldn't want you to spread it around. Folks might think I popped a mainspring. But I felt I had to tell somebody."

"I'm glad you did, Cecil. You've saved me a lot of legwork."

"Are you thinking the same thing I'm thinking?"

"You know what they say about great minds. Good night, Cecil."

Back in the Bentley Diana had the motor running and the defroster on. It wasn't raining nearly as hard, but it was getting colder. "Any luck?" she asked.

"We're a lot closer."

"I hope we're there because we're at the end of the list— at least, at the end of my memory." She turned the fan down a notch. "There *is* one other person, but she's not on the list."

"Who's that?"

"Si Buckles' nearest living relative."

"*Ruth* was there?"

"She came and went, but she was there . . . long enough to view the body."

"I wonder why she didn't want me to know?"

"Why don't you ask her?"

At home Ruth opened a jar of pickles, took a long look at them, screwed the lid back on, and put the pickles in the refrigerator. "Okay, I was there, so indict me."

"I just wondered why," I said.

"I don't know why, to be honest. I had no use at all for Si Buckles the man. I mean that. If he'd set foot in my house, I'd have called the exterminator. But he stayed with me one summer when he was five. It was the year his father died, and he was a pretty sad little boy. We never got close. I couldn't make myself. Even then there was something about him that grated my soul. Well, one night he was catching fireflies all by himself, and he brought them in to show them to me. I nodded and went on about my business—I was knitting, I think—while he just stood there like a statue. Then he began to bawl—not making a sound, just big tears that kept rolling down his cheeks. I tried to get him to stop, and when I couldn't, I sent him to his room and let the fireflies go." She was looking away, somewhere into the past. "So when I walked into that mortuary, I didn't see Si Buckles the man lying there. I saw a five-year-old boy with his hand out. And I touched that hand one last time for all of us who should have and didn't." She turned to me, her eyes wide. "The hand was *warm*, Garth, as *alive* as yours or mine."

"Thank you, Ruth."

"Whatever you do, for God's sake use good sense."

"I will."

Diana sat in the driver's seat with her eyes closed. I pecked on the window. "Yes?" she asked, rolling the window down.

"I hit the jackpot."

CHAPTER 13

Diana and I sat in her family room before a fire. The coffee in my cup was cold, and the fire had shrunk to a small, yellow flame that licked feebly at the heart of the log. Turning to me, she said, "I don't want you to go."

"I'll be fine."

"Then why won't you take me along?"

"It's cold and wet, and there's nothing for you to do but watch. You'd be miserable."

"You're protecting me, isn't that it? You're afraid of what you might find?"

"I don't know what I'll find. But I'll feel better if you stay here."

"Why don't you at least wait until morning?"

"What if someone sees me? It might be hard to explain."

"Get a court order to exhume the body."

"That takes time—time I'm not sure I have. Which brings me to another thing. I don't want you to stay here tonight alone. I'm sure Ruth would like your company."

"Garth, what about you?"

"Nothing will happen to me."

"How can you be so sure?"

"It's something I know about myself. I might be a duck, but I always land on my feet."

"Did I miss something?"

"I'll have Ruth explain it to you."

"At least, call Sheriff Roberts and tell him where you're going."

"I did. He's not home."

"Did you leave word?"

"No one's home." I got her coat and helped her put it on. "I know it's useless to say, but don't worry."

"You're right. It's probably the most useless thing you've ever said."

I let her and the Bentley off at home, picked up some tools, climbed into Jessie, and drove toward Navoe Cemetery. The rain had nearly stopped and now came enclosed in waves of fog that sprayed against my headlights and cut my vision in half. I turned on the heat and pushed the fan to high, but I was still cold. Turning onto the gravel, as the road narrowed and the trees closed overhead, I began to tap my fingers nervously on the wheel, and by the time I got to Broken Claw, hunched there in the fog like some primeval lizard, the wheel was slick with sweat.

Tillie's house was dark, no lights burning in any of the rooms. I checked my watch. Eight o'clock. I wondered where she was. Stepping outside the car, I heard movement in the underbrush and caught a glimpse of what looked like her Walker hound skulking behind a blackberry bush. I tried to call him to me, but he whimpered once and slipped deeper into the woods. Maybe Tillie was in bed.

I drove on and parked at the entrance to Navoe. As the fog wrapped a white scarf around the white stones, my thoughts went back to Wyandotte—the blackened orange bricks and the initials R.C. + D.C. with the X slashed through them. It all seemed part of an invisible chain that had its end here. If there *was* a connection, I was about to learn it.

When I stepped outside and turned on my flashlight, I discovered I'd forgotten to change the batteries and had only a dim, yellow ray to see by. I turned it off and began to walk, angling across the cemetery toward Si Buckles' grave. Catching an unseen root with my toe, I pitched headlong into a tombstone, as shovel, spade, and flashlight went flying. I lay for several seconds before I realized what had happened. Then I couldn't find the flashlight. Crawling on my hands and knees in a tightening circle, I felt something hard and smooth and bonelike against my shin. Hoping it was the flashlight, I picked it up and tried the switch. Nothing. I alternated the batteries and tried again. It worked, but only put out the same feeble yellow light as before.

I finally found Si Buckles' grave and cleared away the dead flowers on top of it. My foot resting on the spade, I considered for a moment what I was about to do. Some people live their fantasies. I was living my oldest nightmare. I pushed on the spade. It cut easily through the soft, damp earth.

Using the spade to shape the hole and the shovel to crumb the loose dirt, I worked my way down. The first couple feet went well, as I pushed and swung with an easy rhythm. Then I felt a familiar foe grip the end of my shovel and hold on. It was blue clay, and it stuck like gum, making me pay for every inch, as the fog settled in, rain and sweat mingled and ran into my eyes, and the hole grew slowly around me like the widening jaws of a trap.

A twig snapped a few feet away. I stopped shoveling and listened, but heard only the rain crinkling the dead flowers. I started digging again. I stopped. Just the rain, as before.

An hour later, I felt the spade strike the casket for the first time. I worked harder now, trying to make enough room to open the lid. Suddenly every muscle drew tight, and I could hear my heart in my temples. I was being watched. Slowly straightening, I looked up to see Tillie's Walker staring at me. I set the spade down and spoke as gently as I could. "Come here, boy. What's the matter?" He took a hesitant step. "Come on!" His tail wagging, he'd started for me when he stopped and stiffened, as the hair on his back bristled and his lip curled into a snarl. He growled and jumped back, away from something I couldn't see. "It's all right, boy. Where's Tillie? Where is she, boy?" He continued to back away, growling with each step. The last I saw of him, he whirled and slunk into the fog.

Clawing away the last bit of clay with my fingers, I sat down to study the latch of the casket. I couldn't figure it out. Closing my eyes to let my mind rest, I felt my skin start to crawl. No help there. I hit the latch in frustration and heard something trip inside. I tried the lid of the casket. It was open!

Crawling out of the grave, I found the flashlight and turned it on. It still worked. I slid back down into the hole and crouched in the small niche I'd carved for myself. The moment of truth was at hand, but I wasn't sure I was ready for it. Maybe I could take a deferred payment, say sometime in the next millennium or two. Sucking up my courage, I raised the lid of the casket and shined the light inside. I had part of my answer. Hideously drawn in fear, his eyes bulged, his tongue distended, Si Buckles' face spoke of the terror of being buried alive. The velvet lining was ripped from the casket where he'd futilely torn at the lid, his fingers were gouged and bloody, his watch smashed. "You poor sonofabitch," was all I could say.

I climbed from the grave and lay on the ground trying to catch my breath. The flashlight had fallen to one side, and my eyes followed its dim beam to where it shone through a break in the fog. I shut my eyes and looked again. It wasn't possible. It couldn't be. He was there! Si Buckles stood before me! Whirling, I looked back into the grave to make sure. No. He hadn't moved. I turned back and shined the light where he'd been standing a moment before. He was gone! I swung the light in a slow circle as it skimmed the wall of fog. There was no trace of him, not even the thud of a footfall. Yet I'd *seen* Si Buckles. I'd have bet my life on it.

I searched the cemetery for several minutes until my flashlight gave out. Then I had to find my way back to Jessie. It was slow going, and as the fog grew thicker and engulfed me, I fought the panic, the urge to run regardless of direction. Finally I saw the wrought-iron gate and knew I was getting close. In another minute I was inside Jessie, watching the drizzle smear her windshield like bugs on a summer night. I hadn't tried to start her. I didn't have the nerve.

I turned the key. Unn . . . unn . . . unn . . . unn. I gritted my teeth and jammed the accelerator to the floor. "Come on, Jessie!" She fired once, then again. I kept the accelerator down, as she suddenly roared and died. Putting a white-knuckle grip on the key, I tried again. This time she coughed, belched, and ground to a sputtering fire, but when I put her in gear, she died. "Jessie! Damn you!" The windows were now steamed, and I couldn't even see the hood. This was my last try. The accelerator down, the side window open so I could see, I turned on the key and held it there. Unn . . . unn . . . unn . . . unn . . . . . un. Roar! I didn't wait for her to change her mind. I slapped her into gear, digging two furrows out to the road and all the way up the first hill. I was already past Tillie's when I remembered that I wanted to check in on her. I didn't stop, though. I was afraid I'd never get Jessie started again.

It was a slow trip back to town. The fog never lifted, and crossing Broken Claw I drove with the door open just to keep its floor beneath me. But once I reached Oakalla, I could use the street lights as guide posts. I never, until that moment of seeing the first light, realized how good civilization looked to someone who's lost.

Diana met me at the door, and before I could stop her she was in my arms and smeared with the mud from Si Buckles' grave. "Glory be!" Ruth said, coming from the kitchen. "The prodigal has returned!"

Ruth fixed us all a toddy, and when the chill finally left

me, I told them what I'd found in the grave. I hadn't yet told them whom I'd seen standing next to me.

"So Si was buried alive," Ruth said. "I was afraid of that—fool that he was."

Diana set her toddy down and looked at me, her eyes probing. "Did Fran and Phil plan it that way?"

"No. I don't think so. At least, I don't think they intended for him to die. They probably thought they could outwait all of us and then take Si back into town the same way they'd brought him out. But when I stayed talking to Ruben, they changed their minds and left, planning to come back later."

"Then it snowed," Diana said, "making the roads impassible and trapping Si in his own grave. That's a nice bit of irony, isn't it? The last laugh. It costs all of them their lives." She took a drink of her toddy and set it down again. "But why would Si go along with it?"

"He was dying, remember? Or at least thought he was. He really had nothing to lose. He could watch his own funeral, have a good laugh, and when the time came, die happy. He didn't know that Fran and Phil had set him up with the bone disease story." If there even was a bone disease story. By now I was sure Si couldn't have written the diaries. Though whoever did write them seemed to know Si better than Si knew himself.

"But where would he go in the meantime?" Ruth asked. "He wasn't supposed to be dead. He couldn't just disappear."

"There's one possibility," I said. "Phil had a whole floor above the mortuary. It would have been easy to make it livable again. It was Si's old home. It'd have been as good a place as any to spend his last days."

"And when he found out the truth, that he wasn't dying?" Ruth asked.

"I'm afraid that would have been his problem. To hazard a guess, I'd say Fran and Phil would have made him work it out. Wouldn't you, Diana?"

She nodded. "Yes. Fran really did hate him. He wouldn't have shown Si much mercy. And given the chance, Fran would have laughed him out of town."

"So that solves it," Ruth said. "What we've all been suffering from is an overdose of imagination."

"Not quite," I answered, "because I saw Si Buckles tonight."

"You did *what*?" Ruth asked, sitting up on the edge of her chair.

"Tonight, in Navoe, I saw Si walking around."

"If anyone else told me that, I'd want to smell their breath. Are you *sure*?"

"Positive. Ask Diana. She's seen him."

"He's right, Ruth. I'd swear under oath it's Si Buckles."

Ruth glanced from Diana to me. "You don't mind sleeping three in a bed, do you?"

"Except it couldn't be Si," I said, "unless you want to believe in ghosts." Then I had to face what I'd been avoiding. "Santa Claus in April. I should have known then."

Ruth settled back into her chair. "What?"

"What time is it?" I asked.

"Two-thirty," Diana answered.

"Later than I thought." I walked to the phone and dialed Tillie's number, but it didn't ring. The line was dead. I dialed Rupert.

"Hello."

"Elvira, is Rupert there?"

"No. He's out on a call."

"Do you know where?"

"Who is this?"

"Garth Ryland."

"I'm sorry, Garth, I don't. He said it might be a while—something about an ammonia leak."

"When he gets in, would you have him call me at home? It doesn't matter what time."

"Is there something wrong?"

"I'm not sure yet. There might be."

"I'll try to reach him, but I can't promise anything."

"Thanks, Elvira. Do what you can." I hung up and turned to Diana. "Think hard. Did anyone see you give the roses to Fran?"

"No, I'm sure of it." Her eyes clouded a moment. "No, that couldn't be."

"What couldn't be?"

"It's not even worth mentioning."

"Mention it, please."

She turned away, running her hand along the couch. "Ruben saw me at Fran's grave. Everyone else had gone and you were waiting in the car when I knelt, kissed the roses, and threw them to Fran. When I looked up, Ruben was watching me from the edge of the woods. I waved, but he didn't wave back. I thought perhaps he didn't see me."

I lifted the receiver and dialed again. "Who are you calling?" Ruth asked.

"Fritz Gascho."

"Why at this time of night?"

"I need to get into the hardware."

She watched me closely. "What do you have in mind?"

"I'll tell you later. But if Rupert calls, tell him where I've gone."

"And where will that be?"

"Navoe Cemetery." I smiled at Diana, "Do you want to come along for now?"

"Try to stop me."

I wasn't taking any more chances. I put Jessie in the garage and we drove the Bentley. Fritz Gascho met us at the hardware, wearing his winter coat over his pajamas and the earflaps pulled down on his orange hunting cap. "Nice night," he said, watching the mist steam down. "For ducks."

"I wouldn't ask if I didn't need to," I said.

"I wouldn't do it if it weren't you," he replied. We went

inside and he turned on the lights. "The store's yours. Kill the lights and lock up when you go."

"Thanks, Fritz. I appreciate it."

"A card and flowers to my wife would help more."

"What are we looking for?" Diana asked when he'd gone.

"Paint."

"Any particular kind?"

"Green fluorescent."

"The kind that glows in the dark?"

"That's it."

"What made you think of that?"

"A couple things. Rupert said he must have a fluorescent phone number, since that was the only one people could find at night. And Tillie said it looked like foxfire standing by Si Buckles' grave. Now that I remember, the Si Buckles I saw did have an unusual glow."

"What will it prove?"

"I'll show you later."

She started at one end of the paints, while I started at the other. A few minutes later she said, "I think I've found what you're looking for." She handed me a spray can of green fluorescent paint.

"Are there any more like it?"

She studied the shelf where it'd been sitting. "No. But take a look at *this*." There were two rings in the dust the same size as the spray can I was holding.

I smiled at her. "You'll do."

Before we left, I picked up a roll of masking tape and stuffed it into my pocket. We drove to Si Buckles' house. I still didn't like going in there. It reminded me of a crypt.

"See if you can find a flashlight," I said to Diana.

"Where will you be?"

"The bedroom."

"Why do we need a flashlight?"

"Experimental purposes."

Opening Si's closet, I took one of his green plaid shirts,

covered the black lines with masking tape, and sprayed it with the flourescent paint. When the paint had dried a little, I peeled off the tape and put the shirt on. I turned off the light and waited.

"Garth, where are you?" Diana was coming down the hall.

"In here."

"I found a flashlight." She stopped at the bedroom door. "Where *are* you?" She turned on the flashlight and pointed it at me. An instant later the flashlight fell to the floor.

I turned on the bedroom light. "Are you still with me?"

She stood with her eyes closed. "Garth Ryland, if that's you, I'm going to kill you."

"You can open your eyes." She did. I picked up the flashlight and turned it off for the moment. "I'm sorry. It was the only way I could know for sure if I was right. That *was* Si Buckles you just saw?"

"Most definitely."

"I thought so. I didn't remember seeing his face, but I knew it was Si. I didn't know why until I thought of the shirt." Then I remembered that day along Hog Run when I first thought I saw him; it was the shirt I saw then, too.

"But when I saw him it was dark. He seemed to grow brighter when he stepped out from under the security light and started toward the house."

"Tillie said the same thing. She was sure the moon was under a cloud when she saw him."

"How could that be?"

"I'll show you."

We went into the kitchen where I found a roll of aluminum foil. I unbuttoned the shirt, flattened a sheet of foil against my chest, stuffed the flashlight under my belt so that it faced up, and buttoned the shirt. I turned off the kitchen light and turned on the flashlight. The effect was frightening, even when I knew it was coming. I heard Diana gasp.

I turned the light back on. "So now you know how easy it

was to see Si Buckles . . . especially when it was the same shirt in which you buried him alive."

"And under the guilt of wanting him dead? That was it, wasn't it? That's what ultimately drove Fran and Phil to suicide?"

"I think so."

"But who would do such a thing?"

"Ruben."

"Garth, you can't believe that! Ruben would never purposely hurt anyone or anything."

"Let's take a short drive."

The fog had finally started to break up and now came at us in dense patches that slowly opened and closed like a stage curtain. Diana touched my arm as we stopped in front of her house. "Do you remember my leaving a light on?"

"No."

"I was sure I did."

We went inside. One look told us someone else had been there. There was a trail of mud leading from the back door directly to her bedroom. We followed it, turning on each light along the way, but there was no one in the bedroom. The bedroom window was wide open, and there was mud on the sill. I crawled outside into the sponge-soft yard and found footprints leading away from the house.

"What do you suppose he wanted?" Diana asked.

"He wanted you."

"Garth, don't be melodramatic."

"I'm not. I know that five people went to Wyandotte on October 30, 1959. Of those five, four returned to their normal lives. One didn't. Of those four, three are dead. One isn't. Now you tell me what else he's doing here?"

"You don't even know it's Ruben. And what if it is? He's my friend. He's had a hundred chances through the years to kill me if he wanted. If he wanted to so badly, why hasn't he?"

"He might have been biding his time."

"He doesn't even know what time is!"

"Go get your portrait of him."

"Why?"

"I want to prove a point." She brought it to me, and I turned his face toward her. "It's your best, right, you and I both agree?"

"Yes. It's my best."

"Now, look at his eyes and look at his smile. Is that the face of a fool?"

"No. It's the most intelligent face I've ever seen. That's why I painted it."

"Is that a violent face?"

"A very violent face. But, Garth, he'd never hurt me! I know him better than that."

"You don't know him at all. You don't know what twenty years of brooding will do to a man. It eats at his guts and it eats at his soul until he's not the same man anymore. There's no way to tell who he is or what he'll do."

"So what do we do in the meantime, have him hunted down like a mad dog?"

"What do *you* want to do?"

"I want to meet with him, hear his side of the story. Isn't that what you want to do?"

"I'd rather do it alone."

"How do you know I'll be safe even if I stay here. If I'm so fragile, how can you ever trust me alone again?"

She was right, as much as I hated to admit it. "All right. You win. But you're going to have to trust my judgment. If we get in a tight spot, don't argue, just obey."

"That sounds like the perfect contract." Her voice cut so smoothly I hardly felt it.

We drove to Navoe, as the yellow Bentley flickered in and out of the fog like a firefly. Crossing the cemetery, we'd started down the hill behind it when Ruben's shack appeared suddenly through a break in the fog. Both of us stopped at the same time and exchanged glances. Farther on we could hear the north fork of Hog Run churn noisily through a rapids.

We found Ruben's door and knocked. When no one answered, we went inside. A stack of yellowed newspapers and a pile of bark sat beside a small pot-bellied stove at one end of the room, a crude table and chair were in the middle, and Ruben's bed was at the other end. We stood a moment watching the rain drip through the shack's tin roof onto its plank floor. Beside us on an orange crate a kerosene lantern burned with a smoky light.

"I've never seen anything so bleak," Diana said.

"Neither have I." I crossed the room and wiped the dust from a plaque. It was the American Legion Award for the outstanding eighth-grade boy. Beside it were framed certificates for excellence in Latin, chemistry, algebra, and English. Then I read something else he'd framed. I removed it from the frame, folded it, and put it into my pocket. "It makes you wonder, doesn't it?" I asked. "Say you have a brilliant mind and you see things faster, more deeply than other people. Say at seventeen you already realize you're a square peg trying to fit into a round hole, and it hurts—it hurts more than you can say . . ." I turned to Diana. "But there's this girl, this very special girl who's not like all the rest, whom you know you can trust . . ."

"Garth, *stop*."

"Who you know, if she says she'll meet you in the lowest rung of hell, will be there. Who would never lie to you, or set you up for the cruelest kind of joke . . ."

"I didn't know! I swear I didn't know!"

A wave of cool, wet air passed over us. The door was open and Ruben stood in the doorway, as the lantern flickered wildly, drawing the mist to the threshold, then pushing it away, back into the night. He was taller and thinner in here, his cheeks gaunt, his eyes set straight ahead, seeming to see nothing, and his face was smudged with charcoal, white streaks showing in it where the rain had washed through to his skin. I felt Diana recoil, as she reached for my hand. "Hi, Ruben," I said.

"Hi, Mr. Ryland, Diana. Won't you have a seat?" He took off his baseball cap and leather jacket. Beneath was one of Si Buckles' shirts. Diana and I sat together on the bed, while Ruben dragged the chair from the table and sat facing us. "I'll bet you're wondering about this shirt, why I'm wearing it?"

"Among other things," I said.

"I didn't mean to do it," he said smiling.

"Do what, Ruben?" Diana asked.

"Scare Si Buckles to death. I was only trying to let him out. I was in the cemetery when I heard him hollering, and I went over to see what was the matter. It was snowing and blowing so badly I couldn't tell where the sound was coming from at first." His smile broadened. "I nearly went crazy running around that cemetery looking for a way out—I mean looking for a way in. Well, you know what I was looking for. It almost seemed like it was my own mind screaming inside of Si Buckles. I finally found him, though, and I knocked on the lid of the casket.

"'Is that you, Doc?' he asked.

"I didn't answer.

"'Is that you, Doc?'

"It was louder this time.

"'Doc, *please*, you have to let me out. The joke's gone far enough! I'm suffocating in here, Doc! Phil, you out there? I don't want to die like this! Dear God, I don't want to die like this! Dear God, I don't want to die like this!'"

Ruben pulled his chair closer. "I think that's what he said. It was snowing and blowing so hard I couldn't hear exactly. Then he started crying. I really felt sorry for him. I hate to hear anyone cry. Then he started tearing up the inside of the casket. It was an awful sound, his thrashing and crying and begging for somebody to let him out. I couldn't stand it anymore." His gaze leveled on Diana. "I mean you just can't stand there and let someone go crazy, so I opened the lid, and he took one look at me and fell dead." Ruben glanced from Diana to me. "Why do you suppose he did that, Mr. Ryland?"

"I don't know, Ruben."

"I know I'm ugly, but I never thought I'd scare anyone to death."

"You're not ugly," Diana insisted.

"It's nice of you to say that, but you don't have to. I don't mind. Out here it doesn't matter what you look like." He stared at Diana until she turned away.

"What did you do then?" I asked.

"I checked him over. He was dead all right. It seemed a shame, seeing how he was always cutting up and acting the fool. He wasn't at all like me. No, I take things seriously, too seriously for my own good. Diana was like that," he said, as if she weren't there. "I've never seen a girl so serious about life. She was always wanting to know this or that and asking me questions I was hard put to answer. It made me feel good to be around her."

"Did Fran and Phil ever come back for Si?" I asked.

"What?" His smile was centered on Diana.

"The night of the snowstorm, did Fran and Phil ever come back for Si?"

His gaze stayed with Diana, as his smile deepened. "Yes, they came back the first thing the next morning. I was standing at the edge of the woods watching. Phil was telling Fran they should never have done it and Fran was telling him to shut up. When they opened the casket, Phil was real upset. He kept saying he couldn't live with this, not after what happened at Wyandotte." I felt Diana stiffen, but Ruben seemed not to notice. "Fran said he was glad to be rid of him, and he really didn't care how. Maybe now he could have some peace in his life. Phil called Fran a murderer and Fran just laughed. Fran said he deserved to be called much worse than that. It was one thing to take a man's life, it was another to take his girl and make a fool out of him for all of the world to see."

"Fran said *that*?" Diana asked.

"It was still blowing hard, I thought that's what he said. It made sense to me." He glanced out the window at the fog. "Then they left. I helped push them out of the snow. They never saw me. I'm good about that."

"Did you come on in to town?" I asked.

"Yes . . . no, not that night."

"When *did* you come into town?"

"Garth, this isn't an inquisition," Diana said.

"Hear no evil, see no evil, *speak* no evil," I answered.

"It's okay," Ruben was smiling at us like a genial host. "I know I did wrong, taking Si Buckles' shirt like I did and spraying it with that glow-in-the-dark paint. But it seemed like a good joke to me. Here, Fran and Phil were always the ones having a good time, while I was studying, trying to make something of myself. And they always got the girls, too. I never could figure it out. As smart as some people said I was, I never could figure it out why it never mattered how smart you were, only if you could make people laugh. So I thought I'd try it once—you know, play the fool like Si Buckles always did. And who better to play the fool than Si Buckles himself? That's what he was planning to do. I'm sure of it. He was going to run around scaring people until he died. I didn't see the harm in taking the joke to its natural end. I didn't tell Fran or Phil, though. That'd spoil it for them."

"Did you bring the diaries when you took Si's shirt?" I asked.

He appeared confused. But I knew better. "No. I didn't know about the diaries, not until I read them in your paper." His smile had faded to a thin line, and his deeply intelligent eyes were never brighter. "But that's something, isn't it, Mr. Ryland, how we spend our lives doing others harm and never are called to account? Then one day a record appears, a record of our life, written in our own hand. If somebody else had written it, no one would believe it, but since it's ours, no questions are asked, and our life is laid open for everyone to see." His smile returned. "Tell Mr. Gascho I'm sorry about his windows, and as soon as I get the money, I'm going to pay him for them and the things I stole."

"Garth, we've taken enough of Ruben's time," Diana said.

"Oh, I don't mind," Ruben answered. "It's kind of nice to have people call here. It's the first time I can remember."

"The shirt, Ruben, why are you still wearing it?"

"It's the warmest thing I've got, Mr. Ryland. I plan to put it away forever as soon as the weather warms up."

"Garth, it's awfully late," Diana insisted.

"We'll go in a minute," I said. I glanced around his shack as the rain continued to drip. "Ruben, have you seen Tillie tonight?"

"No, not that I remember. Isn't she at home? That's where she usually is."

"I couldn't raise her."

—— 183 ——

"I'm sure that's where she is."

"One other thing, Ruben," I said. "Why did you take the roses to Diana? Didn't you know it would frighten her?"

"I'm sorry about that. I really am. I saw how much it hurt her to leave them there, so I thought I'd bring them back to her. I forgot who I looked like and when I heard her scream, I thought she was in trouble and I tried to get in to help her. It was then I remembered the shirt and saw I was the one she was screaming at."

"Satisfied?" Diana asked me.

"Ruben, were you in town earlier tonight?" I asked.

"No, I was out walking around. It gets lonely here sometimes with just the dead for company."

"Are you sure? I thought I saw you."

"I'm sure, Mr. Ryland."

"I thought I'd ask. Thanks, Ruben, we'll be going now."

"Why don't you let me fix you some tea first?" he asked. "There's some mint growing down by the creek."

"Why don't you," I replied.

"Garth, do you know what time it is?" Diana asked.

"What difference will another hour make?"

"That's right, Mr. Ryland, I won't be gone long." He put his cap and jacket back on.

As Ruben stepped outside, I grabbed Diana by the wrist and led her to the door. "Garth, what are you doing?"

"I'm getting us out of here." I heard Ruben moving through the underbrush toward the creek. "Let's go!"

"Why?"

I was trying to drag her, but she wouldn't go. "He knows what he's doing. He has all along."

"How do you know?"

"A lot of reasons, but one is all we have time for." I took the piece of folded paper from my pocket. It was the missing page from Si Buckles' first diary. "Read it, but hurry."

I thought back over all that had happened from the night at Wyandotte twenty-four years ago: the burning of the Hull House; the years he spent writing Si Buckles' diaries; the months in the second-floor room of the mortuary listening and waiting for his chance; the entire sequence of events that finally brought Diana to his doorstep. "Yes, he planned it all."

"And he plans to kill me next, right?" She no longer smiled.

I looked outside, as the light from Ruben's flashlight swung our way. "Hurry!"

The hill behind the cabin was wet and slippery and a hard climb. After crawling on our hands and knees the last few feet, we'd started across Navoe when I heard a familiar sound behind us. It was the click of a shotgun barrel snapping into place. In the fog I couldn't tell where it came from, but it was close.

By now I knew the cemetery well, and I used the headstones to guide us out. Even in the fog, the Bentley was easy to see. I was more than glad we brought it. Easing the door open, we slid inside. I turned on the ignition and pushed the starter. Unn . . . unn . . . unn . . . unn. No! It couldn't be! "Let's go!" I said, dragging Diana from the car.

"What's wrong?"

"Ruben's pulled a wire."

We were running now, and the gravel crunched loudly underfoot. Stopping a moment to listen, I heard quiet, deliberate footsteps following. I glanced at my watch. Five-thirty. It'd be light before we could ever reach town.

We left the road and started up Tillie's hill. Partway up the hill we found one of her dogs in a broken heap. Another lay dead on the porch. The door of the house stood open and just inside, stretched as in sleep, lay her pet goat with its throat slit. After barring the door behind us, we eased our way through the house and barred the back door.

"What do we do now?" Diana asked.

"We look for Tillie."

We searched from room to room, but Tillie wasn't anywhere to be found. "Maybe she's somewhere outside," Diana said.

"No. She's right under your big feet," Tillie answered from under the house. "If one of you'll move, I can get out of here." We stepped to one side, as she pushed open a trap door and crawled out. "It's my alien shelter," she explained. "I figured before they could carry me off they'd have to find me first." She hugged both of us. "Lord, you're a sight for sore eyes! What brings you here?"

"Ruben." I said. "He's after us. I was afraid he might have killed you."

"No. As you can see, I'm still here. Not that he didn't try, though." She nodded to the goat, "Billy's dead. Ambrose, my pig, deserted under fire, and I don't know what happened to the rest of them. I haven't had the heart to go looking."

"Whatever happened?" Diana asked.

"I got too nosy for my own good, that's what happened. I started wondering about some things, like how much Si Buckles' ghost walked like Ruben and why did he always come from the direction of Ruben's shack, so I went poking around his place and saw him wearing that green shirt. I knew then what he was about. I didn't waste any time getting back up here because he can run down a deer if he'd set his mind to it. It was too late, though. I could see that green shirt coming straight up the hill toward me. I didn't wait to see if it was a social call. I bailed out right then. And when I heard Old Bo yelp his last, I knew I'd made the right choice." Her eyes sparkled in the morning dusk. "I guess I could have used the shotgun, but me and Ruben—well, we go a long way back."

"He has your shotgun now?" I asked.

She nodded.

"Is it a single shot or a double barrel?"

"Single shot."

"How many shells did he take?"

"A full box."

"Quail loads?"

"Buckshot."

"That should be sufficient." I looked around the room. "Any other weapons in the house?"

"Not a one. Unless you count my hunting knives?"

"Do any of them have a loose handle that I can get off easily?"

"No. But I have a spearhead I found along the creek several years back . . . It's razor sharp if that'll help any."

"That'll do. I'll also need a bamboo pole and some fishing line if you have it."

"I do."

I heard something heavy slam against the back door. "I think he knows we're in here."

"That'd be my guess."

Tillie brought me what I'd asked for, and using Ruben's old Boy Scout knife, I split the bamboo pole, then inserted the flint spearhead into the split and secured it with the fishing line. As I stood and tested the spear for balance, I thought of Frost's words, "like an old-stone savage armed." But it was better than nothing.

"Garth, what did you mean tonight when you said, 'Santa Claus in April?'" Diana asked. "That's when you knew it was Ruben, wasn't it?"

"I think I can answer that," Tillie said, "since I'm the one who said it first. It *was* Ruben. He was carrying a feed sack and walking toward town."

"Is that unusual?"

"It is in the middle of the night. My guess is that he was carrying Si Buckles' diaries. Isn't that your guess, Garth?"

"Yes. That'd be my guess. He put them in Si's chest and left the key where I'd be sure to find it."

"But if not diaries, what *did* Si keep in the chest?" Diana asked.

"Baseball cards," Tillie answered. "When I was at his place earlier this evening, I watched Ruben burn them one by one. He'd hold each one up to the light before he dropped it into the fire. I could have cried."

Something heavy slammed the front door. "Get down!" I said.

I crawled to the door and listened. All I could hear were some birds chirping quietly. Unlatching the door, I tried to ease it open, but I couldn't. We were barricaded in.

The first shot took me by surprise, as it ripped through the front window, spraying me with glass. A moment later a second shot took out the other window.

"Garth, are you all right?" Diana asked.

"Yes. You and Tillie get under the house."

"What about you?"

"Don't worry about me."

"I don't want to hurt you, Mr. Ryland," Ruben said from outside. "Just send Diana out, and you can leave in peace. Do you hear me, Mr. Ryland? Just send Diana out through a window. She's all I want."

"Ruben?"

"Yes, Mr. Ryland?"

"Why don't you give it up? You've had your vengeance."

"I can't, Mr. Ryland. You see, when I heard Si Buckles screaming from the grave for somebody to let him out, it brought back too many memories, things I wanted to forget, but never could. I suffered, Mr. Ryland. I nearly lost my mind that night. But I didn't, though. I lost something else—I don't know its name, but it's what makes a man go into the mountains and never come out again. Call it love, if you will, love of your fellow man. They took that from me, Mr. Ryland, they and all the others who used to laugh at me. Now, I've paid them back . . . all of them except one. I wanted her to be last. I wanted her to live with it like I did."

"She didn't know, Ruben. She didn't know what they had planned."

"She gave me the note herself, Mr. Ryland, the one telling me to meet her there."

"Diana, is that true?" I asked.

"No! I swear it isn't!"

She might be telling the truth. She might not be. It didn't matter now.

"And she was there, Mr. Ryland. How could she be there and not know? She made a fool of me. I trusted her, and she made a fool of me." He was moving closer. "Mr. Ryland, it's going to be light soon. You're going to run out of places to hide. All I want is Diana. I have no quarrel with you. You've always done right by me."

"Ruben, you haven't killed anyone yet. Why don't you let it end here?"

"I killed Si Buckles. I choked him with my bare hands. That gave me pleasure, Mr. Ryland, more pleasure than I ever imagined." He'd stopped a few feet away. "If they'd stopped with me, I might have forgiven them. But they didn't. They went right on like it never happened. That's when I decided that someday they'd have to know just what it felt like." He was moving again. "All those years, Mr. Ryland. All those years I could have had. They're gone. How can anything make that right?"

It was growing lighter outside. The fog was nearly gone, and I could distinguish the black silhouettes of the trees. I heard the porch creak and glanced up to see Ruben at the window. "It's time, Mr. Ryland. Send her out."

"I'm already here." Diana's voice came from outside.

Tillie peered out from under the house. "How did she get out there?" I asked.

"Through the root cellar. I tried to stop her, but she had her mind made up."

"You wanted me, Ruben. Here I am."

Ruben turned slowly, cocking the shotgun as he did. "I'm sorry, Diana," he said. "It'll happen fast from now on. You won't even feel it."

I sprang, driving straight for him with the point of my spear. Then he turned and smiled at me for the last time. It was a brilliant smile, filled with irony and the promise that was once his. In that instant I knew the full tragedy of Ruben Coalman. Not just for him, but for all of us. His was a mind that could have harnessed the sun.

He never tried to move. The spear pierced his chest, as he sagged slightly and dropped the shotgun. Falling to his knees, he ripped out the spear and threw it aside. I crawled out the window to him and tried to stop the flow of blood with my hand, but he caught my wrist and held my hand away. "It's better this way, Mr. Ryland," he said. "It was never much fun being Ruben Coalman . . . either one of us." His voice faded as his lifeblood spilled out. "One favor, Mr. Ryland. When you print my story, all I ask is that you set the record straight. Let it be known that Ruben Coalman was no fool . . ."

Diana knelt beside me and took Ruben in her arms, rocking him like she would a child. He looked up at her, smiled in recognition, and closed his eyes. "Ruben, I didn't know. *Please* believe me when I say it. I didn't know."

But Ruben didn't hear. He was dead.

I rose and walked to the edge of the porch. Through the trees I saw a sliver of sky and the long, red streaks of morning. I couldn't look at Ruben. His face was too gentle, serene, lifeless. He always called me Mr. Ryland. I'd remember that. And I'd remember his brooding eyes and haunting smile until the day I died. I'd also remember that I was the one who'd killed him. For God's sake, Ruben, why?

Diana joined me, and we leaned together for strength like the sides of an arch. "Will you be all right?" she asked.

"I don't think so this time."

"You didn't know. You couldn't have known this would happen."

I walked to where Tillie's shotgun lay on the ground. I picked it up. "I should've known. He loved you, Diana. I should've known he'd never hurt you." I broke the shotgun open. I expected it to be empty. Instead, a shell jumped out at me and thumped on the ground.

"What were you saying?"

"Nothing." I knelt and examined the shell. It was a twelve-guage, magnum, double-aught. At close range it would cut you in half. I looked at Diana and shuddered.

"Tillie," I said, "we're going to find a phone and call Sheriff Roberts."

She sat on the porch, tucking her feet under her skirt. "I'll stay here with Ruben. As I said, we go a long way back."

"Long enough to know his true mind?"

"How long is that, Garth . . . for any of us? I'll remember Ruben as I want to, and you can remember him as you want to, and maybe between us his truth will be served. I don't know. I'll miss him. Every time I look across Navoe and he's not there, I'll feel a little older, a little lonelier. Some people you miss. Some people you don't. That's as close as I can come to answering you."

I took Diana's hand and we started down the hill just as the sun broke over the horizon.